Reading
BOROUGH COUNCIL

Reading Borough Libraries

Email: info@readinglibraries.org.uk
Website: www.readinglibraries.org.uk

MCLOUGHLIN, Coleen   PET
Rock That Frock!

To avoid overdue charges please return this book to a
Reading library on or before the last date stamped above.
If not required by another reader, it may be renewed by
personal visit, telephone, post, email, or via our website.

Coleen
Style Queen

Rock That Frock!

HarperCollins *Children's Books*

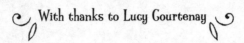

With thanks to Lucy Courtenay

First published in Great Britain by HarperCollins *Children's Books* in 2008.
HarperCollins *Children's Books* is a division of HarperCollins *Publishers* Ltd.
77-85 Fulham Palace Road, Hammersmith, London, W6 8JB.

1

Text copyright © Coleen McLoughlin 2008
Illustrations by Nellie Ryan/EyeCandy and
Nicola Taylor NB Illustration 2008

ISBN-13 978-0-00-727741-4
ISBN-10 0-00-727741-5

The author and illustrator assert the moral right to be
identified as the author and illustrator of the work.

Printed and bound in England by Clays Ltd, St Ives plc

One

OK, so a bit of advice here. Never go dancing in a strapless top. Especially if you're at the gig of your absolute favourite band, Bubbly, whose songs make you want to go mental on the dance floor.

"You OK, Coleen?" my mate Mel yelled over the thumping music. She looked fab in a Bubbly T-shirt and a new pair of skinny jeans, with her huge cloud of hair catching the lights.

"I'm great!" I yelled back, dancing like crazy while

5

hanging on to my top with both hands. I had a feeling I looked a bit weird.

All the old beardy-bloke portraits started wobbling on the Town Hall walls as Bubbly – the best band *ever*, by the way – revved up for the chorus of their massive hit, *Wave Like You Mean It.* The kids packing out the Town Hall floor started going even crazier, waving their arms madly in the air. I clutched my top with one hand and waved desperately with the other, wishing for the millionth time that I'd worn something a teensy bit more sensible.

"Get your arms up, Coleen!" my other mate Lucy laughed, her long hair flying all around her like a huge blond halo. As usual, she was plainly dressed in a neat little blouse and ironed jeans. "C'mon, go for it!"

"*Wave, wave, wave like you mean it,*" sang the band, along with the whole of the audience. "*If there's a*

better way, I ain't seen it; wave, wave, wave like you mean it, whoo!"

The lead singer of Bubbly is called Deena. She looked totally wicked in her hot-pink skinny jeans, and I completely adored the cropped cardie she was wearing over a black top. Her hair was streaked all these different colours, and she was jumping around in high-heeled gold shoes like she was wearing trainers. You've got to admire that. The two girl guitar players, Lori and Jammie, were doing these leaps from side to side like a pair of funky kangaroos – Lori flicking her long, jet-black hair from side to side and Jammie's bleach-blond quiff gelled straight up into the air.

"If there's a better way, better way, we ain't seen it, whoo!" Deena sang, pumping the air with her hands.

The song thundered on through Lori's final guitar solo and a *crash-crash-crash* from the drummer,

7

Belle, with her snaky blond plaits. This really was my last chance. Heaving my top up, I clenched the middle bit between my teeth and threw both my hands into the air, just as...

"Thank you!" Deena yelled as the song died away and the audience went bananas.

Typical.

"Hartley," Deena went on, "you're the best home town ever!"

I forgot about my top troubles at that and screamed, "Yay!" along with the rest of the hall. The whole of Hartley was dead proud of Bubbly. They had even gone to school at Hartley High – though that had been a bit before my time.

After two more encores, we all streamed out of the Town Hall, blinking a bit in the low-lying sunshine of the late afternoon. The music had been so loud that my ears were still ringing – plus my head was

8

full of how I was going to recreate Bubbly's look as *soon* as I got home. They were so cool, they were practically frozen!

"Wow," Lucy giggled, pushing back her hair. "That rocked."

"Wicked," Mel agreed as she wiped her forehead.

"What?" I said to Mel, sticking a finger in one of my ringing ears.

"WICKED!" Mel roared at me.

"Trust Mel 'the Mouth' Palmer to be showing off on the Town Hall steps," said a snidey voice behind us.

We turned round to see Summer Collins, Hartley High's worst specimen, coming out of the gig. Her two best mates, Hannah Davies and Shona Mackinnon, were standing next to her. To say that Summer and her mates weren't my favourite people in the world would be like saying chocolate-flavoured lip gloss was just OK: in other words, a

9

massive understatement! Unfortunately they were all in our class so we had to live with them – like you have to live with a crop of zits when they pop up on the end of your nose.

Today, Summer and her pals were all wearing exactly the same pink hoodies and sparkle-encrusted trainers. They are so *sad*!

"Uh-oh," I said, not missing a beat. "It's the Three Clones." I whipped my head around, pretending to look scared. "How many more of you are there? Are you taking over the world?"

Summer tossed her hair. "Come on, you two," she said to Hannah and Shona. "We've got better things to do on a Saturday afternoon than talk to a bunch of losers."

"So have we!" Mel called cheerily after Summer as she stalked away with her friends in tow. "Like finding the scientist who cloned you all and asking

10

him really nicely to stop before he makes any more!"

"Anyone fancy coming with me for a drink?" Lucy said when I'd finally stopped laughing. "I'm meeting Frankie."

The Frankie in question was Frankie Wilson. He had a brother in our class – Jimmy – and Lucy had just started seeing Frankie after a massive mix-up... but that's another story!

"Can't," I said, catching my breath. "Stuff to do."

"Don't tell me you're going to do your homework," said Mel in horror.

"There's tomorrow night for that," I said, waving my hand to kill the homework ghost before it ruined my weekend. "No," I continued, "I have *fashion plans.*"

I'm famous for my fashion plans. It doesn't take much to inspire me, and then I'm away on my Next Big Thing.

"Ooh," said Lucy. "What are you planning?"

11

"Think Rock Chick," I said, tapping my nose. "It's my new inspiration. When you see me tomorrow, you won't recognise me!"

We were going to the car-boot sale in Hartley's central car park the next day. It's world famous – at least, in Hartley. There are always bargains galore, and there's nothing I like more than a bargain. We do it every month without fail, and it's the best fun ever.

"What about you, Mel?" asked Lucy.

"I've got to get tea on for Mum," said Mel. "Besides, I'm sure Frankie doesn't want me tagging along."

"He wouldn't mind," Lucy said. "But see you tomorrow then."

"Sure. Ten o'clock, Hartley central car park," Mel said, nodding. "See you there!"

"Hiya!" I shouted as I came through the door and tossed my bag on the hall chair. "Anyone home?"

"Em's doing her homework upstairs," came Mum's voice from the kitchen. "How was the concert?"

"Fantastic," I said happily. "I think I'm going to be in a rock band when I'm older."

Dad appeared in the living-room door, holding a cup of tea. "So," he said, grinning at me. "Actress, fashion designer, model and now rock star. That's a lot of careers to fit in, Coleen."

"They're all the same thing these days," I said, taking the stairs two at a time. "Hey, Mum?" I called, spinning around halfway up. "You know those old black high heels you've got in your wardrobe?"

"They aren't *that* old," Mum said, sounding a bit put out.

"D'you think I could spray them gold?" I asked hopefully, thinking of Deena's shoes.

13

Dad burst out laughing at the sight of Mum's startled face.

"I don't get the point of high heels," my little sister Em said, coming out of her room in one of her old tracksuits. "You can hardly walk in them, let alone kick a ball."

At the grand old age of seven, my little sister is already football mad. I've tried to show her that there's more to life than the offside rule, but she never listens.

"You wouldn't understand, sports freak," I said kindly. "You're too young."

"So are you, Coleen," Mum said, having recovered from the shock. "My black heels are way too high. And besides, they're staying black, and that's that."

I sighed. I'd known that would be Mum's answer, but if you don't ask you never get. I grabbed an old pair of trainers from my cupboard and trotted back downstairs with them. So they weren't heels, but by

 14

the time I'd sprayed *them* gold, they were going to look wicked…

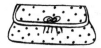

Amazingly, Sunday was bright and sunny. I had been planning to wear sunglasses anyway because rock stars generally do, but it was good to be able to put them on and not have Em teasing me like normal. My newly sprayed trainers gleamed on my feet, and I'd carefully put on my tightest jeans and best black tee with an old cardie I'd cropped right down with Mum's kitchen scissors.

"Now you just need the multicoloured hair," Mel said as I gave her and Lucy a Bubbly-look twirl by the car-park entrance.

"Mum would never let me," I explained regretfully.

Loads of people were around, all lured out by the sun. The whole of the Hartley central car park was

buzzing, music was playing from various parts of the market and there was this festive feeling you usually only get on holiday.

There's something about sunny days that makes me want to spend money – especially at car-boot sales, where the stalls all groan with cheap goodies. Before long, I was the proud owner of two studded leather wrist-straps, a handful of postcards, two CDs and a thin gold belt that wrapped twice around my middle. Then Lucy found a stall selling little china animals and spent ages deciding between getting a cat and a bear.

"Psst," I said, suddenly grabbing Lucy. "Isn't that Ben over there?"

Lucy's big brother was walking down the next line of stalls along from us with his on-off girlfriend, Jasmine Harris. They are both in Year Ten, two years above us.

"Oooh, Ben," Mel said in a silly-swoony voice. "I lurve you…"

"Yeah, yeah," I said impatiently. It was true that I had a crush on Ben Hanratty, but it was hardly news. I'd liked him for what felt like half my life. No – I had a much more important question to ask Lucy.

"So are Ben and Jasmine back together then?"

"Looks like it," Lucy said, shrugging. "Who knows with those two?"

To my horror, Ben and Jasmine were kissing now. I heaved a sigh. One day Ben Hanratty would notice me. But it wasn't going to be today.

"What do you think of this?" Mel said, pouncing on something at the china-animal stall. She held up a little red, white and blue ceramic elephant with a raised trunk.

"For your mum?" Lucy asked, finally buying the cat. Mel's mum collected elephants and had them all over their flat.

Mel nodded, looking delighted as she handed

over twenty pence to the stallholder. "It's exactly the same pattern as this huge one Mum's got by the fireplace," she said, and put the elephant carefully in her pocket.

Lucy's mobile rang. "It's Dad," she said, looking at her screen. "I've got to go, guys – we're going to my gran's for Sunday dinner."

As we waved goodbye, I caught sight of something that made me forget everything else in an instant.

"Look!" I gasped at Mel, pointing to a bright red poster that was fluttering on the side of a nearby car-park ticket machine.

BATTLE OF THE BANDS!

Are you aged between 12 and 16?

Think you've got what it takes to rock?

Make it happen!!

I snatched down the poster and studied it. "Qualifying rounds are in two weeks!" I read. "There's four all across town, with the final taking place in the Town Hall a month after the qualifiers. Contestants must sing a cover version of a well-known song for the qualifying round," I continued, squinting at the tiny print that ran along the bottom of the poster. "Original songs must be performed for the final."

I looked across the top of the poster at Mel. "There's a *trophy*!" I gasped. I'd never won a trophy in my whole life. "You know what I'm thinking?"

Mel goggled at me. "You want to enter Battle of the Bands?" she said. "But we haven't got a band!"

"We can fix that," I said, tucking the poster into my pocket. "Lucy's got the voice, and you and me have got the attitude. What do you reckon?"

"What about a song?" Mel protested. But she was

smiling, so I knew we were getting somewhere.

"We could cover *Wave Like You Mean It* for the qualifier," I said, almost crazy with excitement at the thought of performing a Bubbly song in front of a cheering crowd. "We know it off by heart, don't we? And as for the original song – I'll write one tonight! I mean, how hard can it be?"

Two

"Coleen!" Mum shouted up the stairs. "Bed, *now*!"

I stared hopelessly at the mountains of paper that lay all over my bedroom floor. I'd started about a million songs since tea and hadn't got past the second or third line for each one. I mean, have you ever tried to find a rhyme for "orange"? Forget it! Even "love" is tough to rhyme after a bit.

"Love is a dove in a glove," I said mournfully, staring at my latest creation. "I don't *think* so."

Mum knocked on the door. "It really is time for bed,

21

Coleen," she said. "You've got school in the morning."

"Do you think 'enough' rhymes with 'love'?" I asked hopefully.

"Not really," said Mum, trying to be kind.

"I've *got* to write a song if we're going to win the Battle of the Bands trophy," I said as I pushed back my chair and wandered reluctantly over to my bed. "But it's way harder than it looks."

"You've still got to get through the qualifying round, haven't you?" Mum pointed out. "Don't you think you should be worrying about that first?"

"I want to be prepared," I yawned, snuggling down.

"Prepare for school by sleeping," Mum advised, tucking me in. "Night, love."

Something niggled vaguely in the back of my head as I tried to settle down and stop rhyming things in my mind – something I should have done... But I was too tired to work it out. I slid into a weird

22

dream-world of doves in gloves instead. It wasn't the most restful night of my life.

"Earth to Coleen!" Mel poked me in the side ten minutes into our maths lesson the following day. "Anyone in there?"

"Hmph?" I said, my eyes flying open.

"You fell asleep, didn't you?" Lucy said, looking at me with wide eyes.

"This *is* maths," Mel pointed out. "You can see Coleen's point."

"Of course I didn't fall asleep," I said at once, though I had a nasty feeling that I had. "I was just – daydreaming."

"Coleen?" Mr Hughes the maths teacher was looming over me, holding out his hand and looking at me in this enquiring way.

"Hi, Mr Hughes," I said, shaking his hand. I was still only half awake, to tell the truth. The class roared with laughter. It took me a couple of seconds to work out what was so funny.

"Your homework, Coleen," Mr Hughes repeated. "Do you have it for me?"

The bell of doom rang through my head with a mighty *bonnggg*. Last night's niggling thought… *homework!* Everything flooded back to me. We were supposed to work out percentages on a list of revised recipes – you know the kind of thing, how much extra fruit you have to add to an apple pie to make it stretch to six people instead of four like the recipe said. I'd planned to do it on Sunday night. But the Battle of the Bands poster had totally knocked it out of my head. And I'd wasted my Sunday night thinking about doves in gloves.

"You know, Mr Hughes," I said, desperately fishing

24

around for a decent excuse, "there's a funny story about my homework."

"Don't tell me," said Mr Hughes. "Your dog ate it."

Summer Collins wasn't even *pretending* not to laugh. She and her mates were cackling like chickens as I felt my face flood with heat. Mel and Lucy gazed sympathetically at me as I floundered about.

"Not exactly," I mumbled. "I mean, Rascal did once eat ten quid out of Dad's wallet so he obviously likes the taste of paper – but… well… the truth is…"

"You didn't do it," Mr Hughes said with a sigh. "Am I right?"

I could see it was no good. "Yes, sir," I said sheepishly.

Mr Hughes shook his head. "I'm sorry, Coleen," he said, "but you know what that means, don't you?"

I nodded sadly. Detention. I hadn't had a detention in *months*. How could I have been so daft?

"Tomorrow afternoon," said Mr Hughes. Summer

and her mates were almost wetting themselves with delight. "Straight after school in my classroom."

I gasped and clapped my hand over my mouth. *Tomorrow?*

"Problem?" Mr Hughes asked.

Oh yes. There was a problem all right. A huge one. It was just my luck that Em's latest footie match was *tomorrow* at four o'clock, not Wednesday as normal. We don't usually go to Em's weekday matches as a whole family, but this was her twentieth match for Hartley Juniors so it was a special one. My parents were *completely* going to kill me.

"No, sir," I said dully. "No problem."

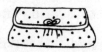

It was hard to concentrate for the rest of the day. I kept picturing Mum's reaction when I told her what an idiot I'd been. It wasn't going to be pretty.

"Let's talk about Battle of the Bands," Mel said, trying to take my mind off things as I gloomily prodded my chicken pie across the plate.

"What battle?" Lucy said, breaking off from this funky little tune she'd been humming most of dinnertime.

We hadn't told Lucy about the poster or our plans for it yet. She'd come into school with her dad that day, so we hadn't seen each other on the bus – and break time was such a rush that we hadn't got round to it. Tearing my thoughts from Mum, I explained as quickly as I could while Lucy's eyes got rounder and rounder.

"So," I finished, feeling more cheerful, "we'll do *Wave Like You Mean It* for the qualifiers and write our own song later for the final. What do you think?"

"Won't there be hundreds of people listening to us?" Lucy asked nervously.

"Yay," Mel grinned.

27

Lucy was looking pale. Even though she's got a brilliant voice, she's never very confident about it.

"You sang in front of all those people at our fashion show," I reminded her. "So you can do it again for sure. And remember – me and Mel are going to be right there singing with you this time."

"The Three Mates," Mel said grandly, sticking her fist in the air. "One for all and all for one!"

"And all for *winning*," I said, beaming as I thought about the cheering crowds that I knew were going to *love* us. "Think of the trophy! We can share it, with each of us having it for a week at a time or something."

"OK," said Lucy reluctantly. "If you really think we can do it."

"I'll register our names, and let's all go over to mine after school on Wednesday," Mel suggested. "We can work on *Wave Like You Mean It*."

She and Lucy then went into this big debate about

28

a dance routine to go with the song. Me? I'd slid right off my happy perch again. I was thinking about how Wednesday came after Tuesday, which came after me having to tell my family tonight that I wasn't going to make Em's match.

"OK," I said, back at home that night. "Here's the thing."

It wasn't looking good. Mum, Dad and Em all stood there looking at me with their arms folded while I rambled through how I'd ended up with a detention the next day. I had a feeling that if Rascal had been able to balance on his back legs, he'd have been folding his arms at me too.

Mum sucked in a deep breath and started on me. "Of all the irresponsible, thoughtless things to do... Em's really been counting on us all being at the match tomorrow, and now you tell us... You knew

about this homework on Friday night and you still hadn't done it by Sunday..."

I tried to picture Mum's words like a big wave that I just had to let wash over me. It would be over in a minute. But it was pretty cold, wet and nasty all the same.

"I'm really sorry," I said humbly when Mum had run out of breath.

Em stalked out of the room. Dad just gave me his Look. I'd have preferred it if he'd drenched me with another wordy wave like Mum's. But the Dad Look was more like the cold wind that blows at you just after you get drenched by the wave, and you realise you forgot to bring your towel to the beach.

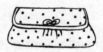

Tuesday afternoon was bright and gorgeous. Trying not to think about Em kicking off in the sunshine

while Mum and Dad shared their usual jokes and a flask of tea on the touchline without me, I stared at the maths questions on my desk and groaned. My homework. Recipes. Percentages. I mean, who *cared* if your apple pie was only big enough for four instead of six? Resisting the urge to write "just serve extra custard", I did my best to work out the problems. The big clock ticked quietly on the wall above Mr Hughes' head, the hands moving as slowly as treacle.

I'd finished the questions after twenty minutes. I still had twenty-five minutes to kill before Mr Hughes would let me go. Staring around the classroom in desperation, my eyes settled on a tattered poster of a beach that hung on the wall beside the door. The picture was old and the beach looked wet and windy, but it was much nicer to look at than Mr Hughes.

I'd like to hear the sea, I thought. *The sea and me…*

Sea. Now *that* was a perfect word for a song. It rhymed with practically everything! Grabbing a piece of paper, I jotted down some random seaside thoughts. The last minutes of my detention whizzed away as rhymes tumbled through my head.

"Thank you, Coleen." Mr Hughes' voice startled me as he took up the paper I'd written my maths answers on. "It's four o'clock. You can go."

I snatched up my lyrics and stuffed them into my bag. "Thanks, Mr Hughes!"

The sea, the sea, I repeated to myself as I barrelled out of the door. The words bounced through my head in a thumping rhythm that had come out of nowhere: *ta-dum, ta-dum, ta-diddly-dum, ta-diddly-diddly-diddly-dum…*

The way from Mr Hughes' classroom to the main corridor takes you past a row of music practice rooms. Kids sometimes work in them after school,

 32

practising for music lessons or just jamming for fun. I could hear some drums pounding out a rhythm that made me want to dance. Peeping through the glass window in the door of practice room three, I almost fell over. It was Ben.

Lucy had often said how her brother played drums, but I'd never heard him. Trying not to let him see me, I stood out in the corridor and watched as Ben Hanratty whirled his sticks over the school drum kit. *Wham! Wham! Wham!* The ground jumped beneath my feet. It was wicked. I closed my eyes and ran my new lyrics alongside the thundering rhythm that Ben was crashing out. It didn't really work – but it gave me the most incredible idea.

What if we asked Ben to play in our band? How cool would that be? And you always hear about band romances, right? Maybe Ben would take me more seriously if we were in a band together!

As soon as I'd thought this, I sighed and tried to forget it. Ben Hanratty would never play for his kid sister's band. But there again, we had persuaded him to model in our charity catwalk show… *If you don't ask, you never get.*

I moved slowly away from Ben's practice room, so deep in thought about how to persuade Ben Hanratty to join our band that it took about three seconds of staring dopily through the next practice room window to realise that Summer, Hannah and Shona were all staring straight back at me.

Summer flung open the door, nearly scaring me out of my mind. "Spying, Coleen?" she challenged, folding her arms and glaring at me.

"Huh?" I said in confusion.

"If you think sneaking a listen to our song will get you ahead of us in the Battle of the Bands, you can forget it," Summer said. "I heard you and your two loser

34

mates talking about entering at dinner yesterday."

My brain whizzed into fifth gear. Summer was entering the Battle!

"I don't need to listen to your song to win," I said, quick as a flash.

"Let's hear you say that when *we* make it through the qualifiers and *you* don't," Summer snapped back. Doing this totally insincere smile, she put her fingers to her forehead to make an L shape and mouthed "Loser" at me, before slamming the door again and pulling the little curtain across the window.

"Says who?" I snapped at the closed door.

This Battle of the Bands was going to be a battle, all right. Summer Collins had just made sure of that!

Three

"So how did Em's match go?" Mel asked the next day as we sat up high on the playground wall and watched the kids flowing around below us like shoals of blue and grey fish.

"Hartley Juniors won," I said. "Em even scored the winning goal. Everyone was so chuffed that they forgot to give me the silent treatment over tea."

Chuffed wasn't the word. Dad had carried Em into the house on his shoulders, forgetting about the lintel over the door. And by the time I got downstairs

with the bruise cream for Em's head,
best mates again – like I'd never had a det
the first place. Families, eh?

"Good one," said Lucy.

We sat quietly for a bit and watched the playground. There's always something to see. A game of rule-less football, maybe, or some complicated game that involves lots of screaming and running around. Some really loud yelling seemed to be coming from the far corner of the playground near the basketball nets. Loads of Year Tens were all clustered together, cheering about something. I craned my neck to get a view of what was happening.

"You'll never guess what," I said suddenly, almost falling off the wall as I saw what was going on. "Your brother's in a fight, Lu!"

Lucy looked shocked. "What? Where?"

I pointed across the playground. Ben could now

be clearly seen. He was rolling around on the ground with his fists hammering at someone.

"I don't believe it!" Mel squealed as the teachers on duty realised what was going on and started legging it towards the fight. "He's only fighting Dave!"

"Dave Sheekey?" Lucy echoed in disbelief. "But he's Ben's best mate!"

"They don't look much like best mates to me," I said, watching as Ben and Dave got to their feet with their arms still locked around each other's necks. I could hear Dave pleading with Ben about something. Jasmine was running up and down, wailing at them both to stop.

"Give over, mate!" Dave yelled, pushing at Ben's hands. "It's just a rumour, yeah? I'd never – *oof…*"

Ben had barrelled into Dave again, knocking him to the ground like a ninepin. Now the whole playground was surging towards the fight like paperclips towards a magnet.

 38

"BREAK IT UP!" Mr Bulford the deputy head teacher roared at Ben, seizing him by the scruff of the neck and hauling him on to his feet while our form teacher Mr Andrews pulled up a relieved-looking Dave. "Hanratty, Sheekey – my office, *now*!"

"Mum's going to go mental!" Lucy wailed as we all wriggled off the wall and rushed over to join the throng of kids all pushing around Dave, Ben, Mr Bulford and Mr Andrews.

Rumours and reasons were already flying thick and fast through the crowd. Dave had dissed Ben's mum. Ben had dissed Dave's dad. Dave had tried it on with Jasmine. Jasmine had dumped Ben for Dave. Trying to make sense of it all was impossible.

Things were even worse by the end of the day. If you believed half the rumours that were flying round the Hartley High corridors, Ben Hanratty had been physically carried off the school premises by

Mr Bulford and thrown out of the gates, while Dave Sheekey had broken four teeth and was going to take Ben to court.

"It's so *embarrassing*," Lucy groaned as we left to catch the bus to Mel's after a full school day of crazy speculation. "Everyone's been after me like I know what it's all about."

"Are you totally sure you don't?" I checked as we boarded the bus.

Lucy just gave me this look.

"All right," I protested, waving my hands at her. "Just – you know. Being his sister and that."

"Do you know everything Em does?" Lucy demanded.

I scratched my head. "Mostly, yeah," I said.

"Well, I guess boys are different, aren't they," Mel said diplomatically.

Lucy looked fed up. "Can we drop it now?" she said. "I'm sick to death of talking about my brother."

I sank back against the bus seat as Mel pulled out a bag of sweets and offered them to Lucy to calm her down. By the time the bus had reached the edge of the town centre and was rumbling towards Mel's flat, everything was cool again.

"So," I said, munching through my fifth jelly baby, "what's that tune you've been humming all week, Lucy? You're doing it now, you know. It's totally got on my brain."

Lucy stopped humming. She looked oddly embarrassed. "Nothing," she said. "Just – a tune."

"It's great," Mel said.

"Thanks," Lucy replied.

Thanks? That was a weird thing to say. Unless…

"Did you write it?" I said, suddenly twigging.

Lucy went a bit red. "I didn't write anything. It just sort of… came into my head last week."

My brain immediately went into hyperdrive. "But

41

it's really good," I said in excitement. "We could use it for our original song for the Battle of the Bands. Don't you think, Mel?"

Mel nodded. "It's funky," she said. "It could work – if we had some words for it. Did you do any words, Lucy?"

Lucy shook her head.

"*I* did!" I burst out, realising. "I wrote some lyrics which fit your tune, Lucy. I wrote them in detention yesterday, and they just sort of – came out in your rhythm."

"You really must've had it on the brain," said Mel as the bus whooshed to a halt and we all piled out.

I took the steps up to Mel's flat three at a time, pounding out the rhythm in my head. *The sea, the sea... Ta-dum, ta-dum, ta-diddly-dum...* And as soon as we got through Mel's front door I sang my lyrics to Lucy's tune.

"*The sea, the sea,*" I went, "*the sea and me, the sea is true and wild and free, the gulls may call, the rain*

42

may fall, it don't matter, not at all – you gotta, gotta
stay in reach of paths that take you to the beach!"

It fitted brilliantly.

"I like it," Mel said as I bounced around the living room doing the *gotta, gotta* part again. "Is that bit the chorus?"

"Yes," I panted, flopping down on Mel's couch. "It needs another verse, but that shouldn't be too hard. What do you reckon, Lucy?"

"Not bad," said Lucy thoughtfully. "It needs something, though. A guitar, or drums maybe?"

"Yes!" I pointed triumphantly at my mates. "So how about we ask Ben to drum for our band? The rules say that you can still compete even if your lineup changes – so long as at least two of your band members are the same."

I could imagine Ben pounding out a heavy backing rhythm on his drums as me and my mates

43

sang our song at the Battle final. The audience would go bananas and sing the *gotta, gotta* chorus part back at us. It would be wild! But Lucy's next words popped that little dream like a sharp pin in a large balloon.

"Sorry, Col," she said. "Ben's already entering with Jasmine, Dave and Ali."

That brought me down off my little rock-star cloud. "Really?" I said in disappointment.

"You didn't honestly think we'd be able to get Ben to play for us, did you?" Mel said. "There's no way any self-respecting Year Ten would play in a Year Eight band."

"That's what we said about Ben and his mates helping our Year Eight fashion show," I reminded her. "And look what happened. We totally pulled it off, with a little teamwork and persuasion, right?"

"Yes, but Ben wasn't already entered in that," Lucy

reminded me before I got too carried away. "He wouldn't let his friends down on something like this."

"Aha, but perhaps they won't be entering now because of Ben and Dave's fight today?" I said hopefully.

"Don't count on it, Coleen," Lucy said, shaking her head. "Not until we know for sure what that fight was about. You know what boys are like – enemies one minute, friends again the next."

"Let's forget about the final and get on with practising for the qualifiers anyway," Mel suggested.

She went over to the stereo in the corner of the living room and put on her Bubbly CD. Soon we were jumping all over the place. The final was forgotten in the fun of putting together a routine for *Wave Like You Mean It*.

"We have to be original," Lucy reminded me as I tried to do Lori and Jammie's kangaroo leap.

"And *careful*!" Mel squealed as I jumped the other way

and knocked a photo frame off Mel's mum's windowsill.

Mel was one to talk! Halfway through the song she did this wild move that knocked into her mum's huge ceramic fireplace elephant. The elephant didn't break thanks to this last-minute shimmy that Mel pulled off, but it moved. We shifted it back as best we could – it was dead heavy – and hoped that Mrs Palmer wouldn't notice. Apparently the elephant was her favourite thing in the whole flat.

In the end, we practised our routine for about an hour. We worked out pogo jumps, a sidewinder move – that's where you move sideways by putting your feet one across the other – these brilliant air-guitar moves, and this one where you crunch yourself up with one knee raised and your elbows touching your knee before pulling your arms down and out to the side and putting your foot back down with a toss of your head. We couldn't really see how our feet looked

46

as Mel's mum only had a mirror above the fireplace, but we had some real rock-star expressions going on!

The sound of a key in the lock made us all realise the time.

"Hello, girls," said Mrs Palmer, dropping her keys on the hall table and putting her bag down.

"Hiya!" Mel said enthusiastically. "We've done this brilliant dance routine that we've *got* to show you after tea. You…"

Mel tailed off as she clocked her mum's face. Mrs Palmer looked as gloomy as a cloudburst on Blackpool Pier.

"Mum?" Mel said, worried. "Is everything OK?"

"Everything's fine," Mrs Palmer sighed.

Me and Lucy looked at each other. No *way* did everything sound fine.

"Did something go wrong at work?" Mel persisted, helping her mother to take off her coat.

"There was just this promotion that I thought they were considering me for, that's all," Mrs Palmer said, trying to look like she was shrugging it off. "Seems like I was wrong. They promoted someone else." Shaking off the gloom, she smiled bravely at us. "Now, who's for some tea? I've got some lovely ham in today."

It was a weird meal, with Mrs Palmer acting like she didn't really mind about the promotion at work when it was clear that she minded a *lot*. To be honest, it was a relief when we cleared the dishes and Mel suggested that her mum should come and watch our routine.

Mrs Palmer settled down on the couch as me, Lucy and Mel all stood in a line. The Bubbly track kicked in. Jump, jump, jump – and *down*, jump, jump, jump – and *around*, sidewinder all along the carpet and back again with a *yeah!* and a twist. We had our arms perfectly together on the elbows-

to-the-knee move, and Mel even managed to work in a version of the little shimmy she'd used to avoid the fireplace elephant.

"*Wave, wave, wave like you mean it*," we sang as the song pumped up to the finish. "*If there's a better way, better way, we ain't seen it, whoo!*" And on the closing *crash-crash-crash* of the drums we all pogoed into the air, landing back on the carpet more or less together.

Mrs Palmer clapped like mad, looking really pleased as we all panted and grinned at her. "That was brilliant," she congratulated us. Her eyes flickered to the fireplace elephant and she frowned ever so slightly. "Did you move—" she began.

"Glad you liked it, Mum," Mel said loudly.

"Do you think we'll win?" I said, joining the conversation as quickly as I could before Mrs Palmer started asking awkward questions about the fireplace elephant's new position.

49

With one last glance at her elephant, Mrs Palmer smiled back at us. "With moves like that, you're bound to," she said warmly.

Yay! Battle of the Bands, bring it on!

Four

You could've cut the atmosphere in our local youth club with a knife. Not even a knife, to be honest – a spoon would probably have done the trick. It was the day of the Battle of the Bands qualifiers, and the place was totally packed out with rock-star hopefuls.

"Do you really think we're ready for this?" Lucy asked nervously as we shuffled towards the desk where they were taking registration details.

"As ready as we'll ever be," Mel said, trying to sound brave.

"C'mon!" I said, rallying my band members. "Bounce Back rocks, OK?"

Bounce Back was the name we'd given our band. It had just the right mix of fun and rhythm to it. And we looked totally wicked, even if I say so myself. We were all wearing black and gold. Mel had skinny black jeans and a white tee with gold swirls on it. Lucy was totally in black apart from her gold trainers, and I was wearing a gold ra-ra skirt that I'd made from this amazing gold crepe paper that works like material and doesn't tear when you sew it.

I turned around, looking for Mum and Nan. When I saw them standing with Mel's mum and Lucy's parents at the back of the hall, they both gave me big smiles and thumbs-up. Em and Dad were at footie, but Em had done me a card that morning. I took it out of my pocket and read it.

It's the winning that counts, not the taking part!!!!!!!!!!!!!!!!

I wondered if she knew she'd got it a bit wrong, and decided that she probably did. Winning was everything where Em was concerned!

"You've got the CD, right?" Mel checked with Lucy.

Lucy waved the CD at us. We'd done it so we just had the backing rhythms of *Wave Like You Mean It* and we would then sing over the top.

Everyone was milling around in crazy, colourful outfits. Summer and her mates were stood in the corner, giggling in our direction while they adjusted

53

their matching pink dresses (ick!). A couple of young kids were by the door, plastered in goth make-up and looking terrified. They couldn't be old enough to take part, surely? And right in the corner I could see Ben, Dave and Ali prowling around each other like wary tigers. There was no sign of Jasmine. I'm sure Lucy had said she was in Ben's band too.

"You know that playground fight?" Lucy said, seeing me checking out Ben and his band. "It was about Jasmine Harris. Ben had heard this rumour that Jasmine had been two-timing him with Dave."

"No!" Mel gasped. "Seriously?"

Lucy nodded. "That's why he was laying into Dave in the playground."

"Do you think the rumour could be true?" I asked, watching as Ben and Dave started arguing in low voices while Ali looked on in a fed-up kind of way.

"Who knows," Lucy said. "Ben has dumped

Jasmine anyway. That's why she's not here. But at least him and Dave are talking again."

Ben and Dave's voices were getting louder. The kids standing near them were starting to edge away.

"Not sure if I'd call that talking," Mel said. "More like arguing."

We'd reached the registration table. "Names, band name, song," said the bored-looking girl at the table. We told her. She raised her eyebrows a bit when we said our song, but wrote it down anyway.

"What was that about?" Lucy asked as we took our seats in the hall.

Mel shrugged. "Dunno. But hey – it looks like Ben's band is first up!"

Sure enough, Ben, Dave and Ali were climbing on to the stage.

"A big welcome to our first band of the day – Snarl!" boomed a voice down a microphone.

"Snarl sounds about right," I said as the audience cheered and settled down in their seats. Ben was shooting Dave the filthiest looks over his drum kit as Dave tuned up his guitar.

They lashed into their song like they were trying to kill it. Playing bass, Ali tried to keep it together, but Ben was too busy eyeballing Dave to keep to the beat, and Dave was totally off the beat as well.

"Is it just me," said Mel in a low voice, "or are Ben and Dave trying to turn this into some kind of musical duel?"

"Oh dear," Lucy groaned. "I guess they've still not made up."

Ben was battering at his drum kit like a lunatic, totally drowning Dave out every time Dave tried to do anything on his guitar. The song splintered into pieces, finishing all together as Ali flung his bass to the ground and stormed off the stage. Yelling could

be heard backstage as Dave and Ben ran off the platform as well.

"Er – thank you, Snarl," said the voice on the microphone. "Next up, we have Coffin. Coffin?"

"*Coffin?*" I echoed, pulling my thoughts away from Ben's awful performance and shaking my head in disbelief as the band of shivering little goths clambered on to the stage. "What kind of a name is that?"

It turned out that I had been right about their age – Coffin *were* a group of Year Sevens. And as eleven was too young for the Battle, they were ushered off the stage by one of the officials while the audience booed them happily. We then sat through five pretty dismal bands of assorted lads with names like Thrash Bunnies and Kick Mighty, who managed to strangle their songs so much that no one could work out what they were supposed to be.

"The Fashionistas, please?" called the voice on the microphone, sounding a bit dazed by now. "The Fashionistas!"

"This ought to be good," Mel said, perking up as Summer and her mates climbed on to the stage. Summer shot me a glance I couldn't quite work out. It looked like triumph.

"They look awful," Lucy giggled.

Summer had so much hairspray on her head that her long, blond, teased-up locks looked like a cloud of candyfloss. I swear you could see her eyelashes from the back row. Shona and Hannah looked even worse, with bright pink lipstick slashed across their faces like a couple of primped-up dollies.

A familiar-sounding tune kicked in from the speakers. Dumbstruck, we looked at each other as Summer, Hannah and Shona started moving to the familiar sounds of *Wave Like You Mean It* by Bubbly.

58

"I don't believe it!" Lucy squealed in horror.

It was a nightmare. *Summer was doing our song!*

"*Wave, wave, wave like you mean it,*" Summer sang, doing this fluttering thing with her hands.

"*If there's a better way, I ain't seen it,*" Hannah and Shona sang obediently, standing just behind Summer like a couple of robotic backing singers.

My brain was zooming at a million miles an hour. That was why the girl at the desk had raised her eyebrows when we had told her our song – she'd already written it down for Summer! And we were about to get up on that stage and do it all over again? There was no way the audience wasn't going to boo us!

"Did Summer know we were doing this song?" Mel hissed at me, recovering from the shock.

"Please make this all a bad dream," Lucy moaned.

Crash-crash-crash went those familiar drums at

the end as Summer, Hannah and Shona twirled like little ballerinas in a music box.

"They like it," Mel said in a hollow voice as the audience all clapped. "We're dead."

"We're not dead," I insisted out loud. *We're totally dead*, said the little voice in my head. I thought back to the day when I saw Summer, Hannah and Shona in the music practice room. Had I heard them singing *Wave Like You Mean It* then? I was pretty sure I hadn't. Was it possible that *they* had heard *us* and changed their song?

"Good luck," Summer hissed across at me as she walked past our row, heading back to her seat with Hannah and Shona. "You and your little band are going to look *sooo* stupid. Wave, girls. Wave!"

Roaring with laughter, Summer, Hannah and Shona all waggled their fingers at us in these teensy, sarcastic waves. Summer *had* heard us! Of all the sneaky things to do…

 60

"Bounce Back?" called the voice on the microphone. "Bounce Back to the stage, please!"

"What are we going to do?" Lucy squeaked in a terrified voice.

"We're going to get up there and show Summer Collins what we're made of," I said, practically pulling Lucy and Mel out of their seats after me. "Their routine stank. Ours rocks – and don't forget it!"

Up on the stage, I gazed down at the sea of faces. Mum and Nan were a couple of anxious-looking blurs at the back of the hall. My legs felt like jelly. Then a stifled giggle from Summer pulled me out of the panic-zone. There was no *way* I was going to let Summer win this! The opening chords of *Wave Like You Mean It* boomed across the hall as me, Lucy and Mel got into position.

"Yawn!" Summer shrieked. "Be more original, why don't you!"

I grabbed the nearest microphone. "I'd just like to say," I said as the beat moved towards the start of our routine, "first the worst, second the best. Remember that."

Jump, jump, jump – and *down*, jump, jump, jump – and *around...* We moved together perfectly, pumping the air and moving up and down the stage.

"*Put, your, hands, in, to, the, air*," we sang, waving our arms as we pogoed up and down. "*Kick, your, feet, like, you, don't, care. Wave, wave, wave like you mean it...*"

I cupped my hands behind my ears as Mel and Lucy danced beside me, listening to the way the crowd sang the next line back at us: "*If there's a better way, we ain't seen it!*"

"*C'mon, c'mon, c'mon*," we sang, moving into our elbows-to-the-knee move and snapping out again like perfectly drilled soldiers.

"*C'mon, c'mon, c'mon*," the crowd roared back. This

was the first song of the day where anyone had joined in. That had to be good, right?

"*If there's a better way, better way, we ain't seen it – whoo!*"

Crash-crash-crash! went the drums. We jumped into the air in our final pogo while everyone cheered like mad. And then my gold crepe-paper skirt decided that it was bored of hanging around my waist and decided to hit the stage instead, showing my pants to the world. The audience went totally crazy as I grabbed at the skirt with my cheeks burning like a bonfire. They seemed to think it was all part of the routine.

"Nice move, Coleen!" Mel giggled as we bowed to the shrieking room and I nearly died. "Did you plan that in advance?"

Unsurprisingly, Ben's band didn't make it. But somehow, Summer's band got through the qualifiers. So did Thrash Bunnies. And so did we! OK, so it would take a bit of time to live down the dropping-skirt thing. But it was *so* going to be worth it if we went on to lift the Battle of the Bands trophy – and then got to wave it in Summer Collins' face!

Five

We had just four weeks to sort out our song for the Battle of the Bands final, which was going to take place in the Town Hall. I still couldn't quite believe that we'd made it through the qualifiers and would be singing up on the same stage that Bubbly had performed on just a few weeks earlier. Even *more* amazing, one of the Bubbly band members was going to be on the judging panel!

"We're actually going to *sing* in front of a member of Bubbly?" Lucy said, looking dazed as we compared

the letters we'd got, confirming our places in the final.

"You'd better start believing it," I said, folding up my letter and tucking it back into my blazer pocket. "*And* we've still got half a song to write."

Mel was frowning at her letter, but I could tell she wasn't really seeing it. Something had been eating her all morning.

"Mel," I said, "you're supposed to be happy right now. We qualified, didn't we? Anyone in there?" I clicked my fingers in front of Mel's face.

"Hmm?" Mel looked up.

"Come on, Mel," Lucy said patiently. "Time to spill."

"It's Mum," said Mel with a sigh. "She's still really down about missing that promotion. She acted pleased that we got through the qualifiers, but I could tell that she was thinking about her work. I wish I could think of a present that might take her mind off things."

"How about another elephant?" I suggested.

"I can't find one she hasn't already got, or doesn't cost hundreds of pounds," Mel said glumly. "Maybe I need to check out the car-boot sale again in a couple of weeks."

"Listen," I said, thinking on my feet. I knew just the way to cheer my mate right up. "I don't suppose you want to be our band manager, do you?"

Mel looked shocked. "Seriously?" she said, a delighted little smile spreading across her face.

I glanced at Lucy. Did she mind that I'd just sprung this on her? But Lu shrugged at me as if to say, "Why not?"

"Now we've reached the final, we need someone to really organise us," Lucy said out loud, joining in with my spur-of-the-moment plan. "Book practice rooms, boss us around until we're word perfect. That kind of thing."

"I can't imagine why we thought of you," I added, punching Mel gently on the arm.

It took Mel two seconds to think about it. "How do I book a practice room?" she said, looking dead animated as she tucked her letter into her bag. "We've got to get on and finish writing our song. How's dinnertime?"

"Good." I grinned over at Lucy. It was working!

"I mean," Mel went on, "*every* dinnertime?"

The grin fell off my face at that. I had a feeling Mel was going to be good at this job. Maybe a bit too good...

After two dinnertimes in the practice rooms, we had our second verse.

"Well done, Col," said Lucy as I put my pencil down and stared at the finished song.

"I hope it's OK," I said, scribbling an extra couple of lines thoughtfully at the bottom.

"It'll be great," Mel insisted, doing her band-manager thing. "So now we've got our lyrics sorted, all we need is a drummer and a guitarist." She made it sound so easy, like you just had to pop down to the local drummer-and-guitarist shop and take your pick.

"Ben's free now," I pointed out hopefully. To be honest, it was the first thing I'd thought of when Ben's band flunked the qualifiers.

"You may have got Ben to do our fashion show," Lucy said, shaking her head, "but there's no way you'll get him to play drums for Bounce Back."

"If we get his mates involved like we did last time, maybe he'll do it!" I said, wondering how Dave and Ali might look as a pair of backing singers.

"But you saw them at the qualifiers, Coleen," Lucy pointed out. "Talk about World War Three. Ben

doesn't *have* any mates to involve right now. All he can think about is his ex-girlfriend, who isn't talking to him either."

Mel was drumming her fingers on the table, her forehead all furrowed up.

"You've thought of something, haven't you?" I said to Mel, recognising the signs.

"Maybe," Mel said with a slow smile. "Maybe not. Just get ready to follow my lead after Friday morning's assembly and do whatever I do, yeah?"

Friday morning assembly was usually really boring. Mr Bulford read out a couple of notices, a bunch of kids did a bit of music and then we all went to class. I was dying to know what Mel was planning as we all filed in and sat down.

A group of Year Tens were doing this morning's

music. As usual with a Year Ten assembly, Jasmine Harris was sitting up on the stage with a couple of other girls I didn't know. They were all fiddling with their guitars and talking quietly to each other. Automatically I glanced around the room for Ben. He was sitting on the end of a row as far away from Dave as possible, looking up at the stage. The whole world could see that he had this soppy face on as he watched Jasmine tuning her strings. Whatever Dave and Jasmine had or hadn't done, Ben wasn't over Jasmine – it was clear as anything.

After Mr Bulford had finished droning about fundraising events and upcoming exams, the girls started playing. It was pretty good actually. All the guitars were overlapping each other and doing different things which somehow sounded like one piece of music.

As we all jostled to our feet at the end Mel hissed at us, "Follow me."

Mystified, me and Lucy followed her out of the seats as she headed up towards the stage. Jasmine and the other girls were still putting away their guitars.

"That was fantastic, Jasmine," Mel said warmly.

Jasmine looked surprised as we clustered around her. "Thanks," she said, smiling slightly.

"You were brilliant," Mel continued, treading hard on my toes.

"Ouch!" I squeaked. This was obviously where Mel needed us to do what she was doing: buttering up Jasmine Harris like she was a piece of toast. But… she wasn't seriously trying to get Jasmine to join our band, was she?

"Fantastic!" Lucy said, obediently beaming at Jasmine. She'd obviously twigged what Mel wanted from us as well.

"Great," I said, racking my brains for something to say. "Very – Jimi Hendrix."

 72

"C'mon, Jas," said the girl packing up beside Jasmine. "We're gonna be late back to class."

"Hold on, Sita," said Jasmine. She glanced at Lucy. "Do you have a sec, Lucy?" Lucy nodded.

Jasmine leaned in. "Has Ben said anything to you about me?" she asked.

"What kind of thing?" Lucy said, looking confused.

Jasmine stood up. "Nothing," she said. "Forget it. Wait up, Sita…"

"Jasmine?" said Mel quickly. "Listen, we know it's dead cheeky to ask, but – I don't suppose you'd like to play in our band for the Battle?"

She'd said it! I almost gasped out loud.

Jasmine actually laughed. "Thanks, but no way," she said, shouldering her guitar. "I can't play with a bunch of juniors. See you."

"Shame," Mel sighed as Jasmine moved past us. "Ben wondered if maybe…"

Jasmine spun around as Mel left the sentence hanging in midair. "Wondered what?" she demanded.

"Forget it," Mel said breezily. "We'll do without a guitar. Ben's drumming should cover it. Practice room three would probably be kind of a squeeze on Monday and Friday dinnertime for a five-piece band anyway."

"You got Ben to play for you?" Jasmine asked, looking astonished.

"Like I said, forget it," Mel said. "It was too much of us to ask. See you." And we walked away, leaving Jasmine frowning after us.

"HeLLO, nutcase!" I hissed at Mel as soon as we were out of Jasmine's earshot. "Ben isn't in the band! And anyway, why would we want Jasmine?"

"Er, radar to Col. Jasmine just happens to be the best guitarist this side of the Mersey, and anyway, in answer to your question, Jasmine doesn't *know* that Ben isn't actually in our band," Mel pointed out.

"But she'll find out," Lucy wailed.

"Jasmine and Ben aren't speaking, remember?" Mel said, smiling wickedly. "So all Lucy has to do is get to Ben over the weekend and tell him Jasmine's playing in the band. You saw for yourselves: she's still crazy about him. And everyone can see that he feels the same way, even though he dumped her. They'll each do it for sure if they think the other one's up for it."

I gaped at her. "That's the maddest plan I ever heard!" I said. "But I like it."

"Me too," Lucy said, starting to laugh.

"I know," Mel grinned. "And see how I made sure Jasmine knew we'd be rehearsing in practice room three on Monday and Friday dinnertimes?" She clicked her fingers. "Sit back and watch the magic, girls."

It was dead clever. Dangerous, loop-the-loop – but clever. The only problem was: did I really want to see Ben and Jasmine get back together for the

 75

sake of our band? My last faint hopes of a romance with Ben Hanratty would all whoosh up in sad little flames if Jasmine joined. But would it be worth it if we won the trophy?

"Hope you've got clean knickers on today, Coleen," Summer said to me as she and her mates pushed past us in the corridor outside the hall. "The ones we all saw on Saturday were *gross*." Giggling, she wafted her hand across her nose and wiggled off.

Well, that pretty much made the decision for me. I tucked away my little Ben Hanratty dream and started focusing on the contest. Bounce Back *would* bounce back – with a drummer, guitarist and *then* some. We had to win this, or die trying!

Six

It was one o'clock on Monday afternoon, and we were sat in practice room three, watching the door like hawks.

"Ben definitely bought it?" Mel checked with Lucy for about the millionth time.

"Totally," Lucy grinned. "He blew me off at first like we thought he would. And then when I mentioned Jasmine, he went all quiet for a minute before bombing me with loads of questions about her."

77

"Don't tell me," I said with a sigh. "He asked what she'd said about him, right?"

"Yeah," Lucy giggled. "So I laid it on a bit thick, saying that she really wanted to see him."

"So," said Mel briskly, "now all we have to do is wait for them to turn up."

We watched the door for another five minutes. Then ten. Then…

"Hi," Ben said, glancing around the room. He was obviously looking for Jasmine. "Am I late?"

"Hi!" I squeaked, jumping to my feet. *Stay cool, Coleen…*

"So," Ben said, settling down at the drums and clattering his fingers against the cymbals. "Is Jasmine coming then, or what?"

"She said she might be a bit late," Mel improvised desperately. The clock was creeping towards quarter past, and there was still no sign of Jasmine Harris.

5, B

3   2   Pu

4   1   with

5

6. 2 lines of sy

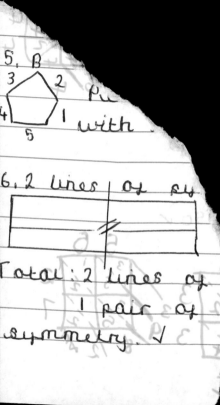

Total: 2 lines of

1 pair of

symmetry. ✓

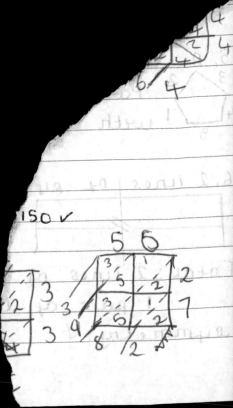

We all sat there like lemons for another couple of minutes. Lucy kept smiling at Ben like a loon, desperate to keep him in the room for a little bit longer. Panicky thoughts ran through my head. Where was Jasmine? What if she wasn't coming? She never said for certain that she'd do it. What if she hadn't remembered which practice room or what time? What if...

Jasmine stood in the doorway, her guitar slung over her shoulder. Her hair gleamed like she'd polished it, and she'd lashed on a load of mascara. I braced myself for the ecstatic reunion of the star-crossed lovers. But as Ben started off his seat like a rabbit, Jasmine glared him down.

"You never said *he'd* be coming," she said coldly, tossing her head in Ben's direction as she put down her guitar and smoothed back her glossy ponytail. Like it needed smoothing – not!

Ben looked shocked as we all gaped at this outright lie. Wasn't she here *because* Ben was?

"Let's not worry about that," Mel said, recovering first. "Great to see everyone. Now, as your band manager..."

Jasmine snorted and flipped open her guitar case. It looked like she was determined to make this difficult. I shot a sneaky glance at Ben to see how he was taking it. He was gazing over the cymbals at Jasmine like a whipped puppy.

"As your band manager," Mel struggled on bravely, "I'd like to explain how we're going to do this. We'll rehearse twice a week for the next three weeks, Mondays and Fridays. We need to learn the song as soon as we can, yeah?" She looked at me. "Coleen? Sing it so Ben and Jasmine can hear it, will you? You too, Lucy."

I felt a blush stealing over my cheeks as Ben and Jasmine both looked at me. Well, Jasmine looked at me while Ben looked at Jasmine. I took a deep breath

and sang through both verses of the song, with Lucy helping me out on the high notes. It sounded pretty weak without any backing music. When we'd finished, we looked hopefully at Ben and Jasmine for feedback.

"And you think we're gonna win the Battle with *that*?" Jasmine said.

"Obviously it needs a bit of work," Mel said. "That's where you come in."

"I liked it," Ben said.

Boing, boing, boing went my heart. My crush liked my song!

"Like *you're* any judge," Jasmine flared. You could tell she'd been dying to have a go at Ben ever since she'd set foot in the practice room. "You judge music like you judge people, do you? You listen and say: yeah, great – but you hear something totally different when someone explains the truth to you and you decide not to believe it?"

Uh-oh. Something told me that Jasmine wasn't talking about the song any more.

"I said I was sorry," Ben began.

"And you think that's enough, do you?" Jasmine stormed. Tears were brimming in her eyes now. "I don't believe you sometimes, Ben Hanratty. This was a stupid idea. I'm sorry I ever came." And she marched out of the practice room with Ben hotfooting after her.

"So," I said, as the sounds of Ben and Jasmine arguing their way down the corridor faded away. "That went well."

"I don't understand," said Lucy, looking confused. "Jasmine had done her hair and everything. It was so obvious she did it for Ben's sake. And then she chewed Ben to pieces!"

"Love is complicated," I said wisely.

"They'll be fine by Friday," said Mel.

Oh yeah? Somehow, I wasn't so sure.

82

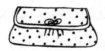

On Friday morning, I almost fainted when Ben stopped us as we got off the bus.

"Sorry about Monday," he said, scratching his head. "I did really like the song, you know. It's that tune you've been humming for weeks, isn't it, Lu?"

Lucy nodded.

"I worked out a beat that would fit really well," Ben continued. "Are we practising today?"

"You still want to do it?" I said in surprise. "What about Jasmine?"

Ben shrugged. "Whatever," he said. "I said I'd be in your band, so that's it. I'm in your band. If you still want me, that is?"

I had a feeling I was staring at Ben like a misty-eyed weirdo.

"Great," Ben was saying as Mel told him the practice room was still booked.

"See you later then."

"Your brother is a *dreamboat*," I sighed at Lucy as we watched Ben walk off through the gates with his head down and his hands in his pockets.

"A dreamboat with a nifty sense of rhythm," Mel said gleefully. "So what if Jasmine doesn't show up today? The song's still gonna sound great!"

You know how I said love was complicated? I don't know the half of it. Because who should join us as we were heading down the corridor towards practice room three but Jasmine Harris. Her mouth was so tightly pressed together her lips had practically disappeared, but she was *here*. Maybe our plans for a five-piece band would work out after all!

When we got to the practice room, we could hear the sound of music drifting out.

"Are you sure you booked it, Mel?" Lucy asked as we stopped at the closed door and looked at each other.

"Definitely," Mel insisted.

"Great," Jasmine sighed, looking anywhere but at Ben.

I knocked on the door. The noise stopped for a second, and the curtain was whisked back from the window. Summer Collins smiled slyly at us through the glass.

"I might have known!" I gasped, rattling at the door handle. It was locked from the inside.

Mel hammered on the door as Summer waggled her fingers at us through the glass. "Hey, Summer!" she shouted. "This is our time!"

"So," Summer purred, "how are you gonna get us out?"

Jasmine marched up to the door and pressed

her nose against the glass. "Get out of our room, squirt!" she yelled.

"What?" Summer said, raising her eyebrows innocently. In the background I could see Hannah and Shona both giggling like idiots. "Sorry, can't hear you." And she whisked the curtain closed again.

"I could kill Summer sometimes," Lucy muttered as we all slumped hopelessly outside the practice room.

"Only sometimes?" Ben asked.

Jasmine laughed. Then, remembering she was still mad at Ben, she stopped abruptly.

"So you still think I'm funny?" Ben said at once.

"Yeah," Jasmine muttered, staring at the ground again. "Funny in the head."

"OK," said Mel, taking charge. "There'll be another practice room we can use. It may not have a drum kit, but we can improvise."

Every single practice room was taken. The clock was

86

nudging towards half past one. It looked like we had just wasted a whole week of important rehearsal time, and there were only two weeks left until the contest!

"This will have to do," Mel said at last.

"You're joking," Jasmine gasped.

I stared at the place Mel had brought us. We were round the back of the kitchens. The stale smell of old cabbages wafted through the kitchen air vents, together with the all-together stinkier smell of the overflowing kitchen bins.

"It's not perfect," Mel admitted, "but no one else is here, so at least it's private."

"I'm not surprised no one's here," said Jasmine in disgust. "It stinks."

"What am I supposed to drum on?" Ben asked, twirling his drumsticks helplessly in the air.

"Use your imagination," Mel said. "There's five perfectly good kitchen bins to work with."

I could feel the giggles brewing. We badly needed to practise, but drumming on the kitchen bins? I mean, seriously?

"OK," said Ben with a shrug. "Let's give it a go. Listen to my beat, then go for it. One, two, one, two…"

I couldn't help it. My snorting giggles were about to get me, big time.

"Hoohoohoo…" I started.

"Stop that stupid honking, will you?" Jasmine told me irritably, trying to get the tune on her guitar.

"She can't," Lucy explained, stopping in the middle of the song as I leaned against the kitchen wall and gasped for breath, my eyes streaming with tears. "We'll just have to wait."

"Hoo," I went. "Hoohoohoo…"

"This is *stupid*!" Jasmine moved towards me – maybe to shake me or something, I don't know. And then she stepped on an old banana skin and her

feet flew up over her head. There was an awful squelch as she landed bum-first on an old tub of yoghurt, which squirted out like pink paint all over her. Her guitar landed with a flump in her lap.

"Hahahahahoohoo!" I was completely doubled over now, as a wave of hysterics overcame me.

Lucy and Mel rushed over to help Jasmine up while me and Ben howled away with laughter. OK, so giggles are pretty infectious – especially when they boom out of yours truly. But maybe Ben shouldn't have laughed just then.

"I hate you, Ben Hanratty!" Jasmine screamed, struggling to her feet in tears. "I quit, you hear? And it's for good this time!" And she ran off around the corner before anyone could stop her.

Seven

"It's all gone wrong!" I wailed at my family over tea that night. "We haven't even rehearsed properly yet and there's just two weeks left, and Jasmine, who wasn't speaking to Ben much anyway, now totally won't come within a hundred yards of him since she slipped on that banana skin and fell in the yoghurt, and Mel is furious with me for laughing – not to mention she's wound up anyway about her mum missing that promotion – and Lucy's really upset because her brother's upset, and—"

"Calm down, Coleen," Dad protested, waving a forkful of cabbage at me. "We can't hear a word. The band's gone wrong?"

"So aren't you playing in the Battle any more?" Em said, looking disappointed.

"It's just a little spat," said Mum. "Bands have them all the time. It'll blow over, love."

I shook my head. "Believe me, Mum, this one won't," I said hopelessly. "And it's all my fault."

Dad was frowning, obviously going through my garbled story in his head. "Jasmine slipped on a banana skin?" he said at last.

"Yes," I sniffed.

"And..." Dad was struggling not to laugh, "then fell in some yoghurt?"

"Pink yoghurt," I said. Like it *mattered*? "A bit even sploshed on her nose."

If you ever wondered where I get my famous

giggles from, you want to see my dad. He gets so bad that he can't speak. He ends up taking a run at the same sentence about ten times, like he's trying to pole-vault over a wall but ends up smacking his nose against it each time instead.

"She slipped… she slipped… slipped…" Dad choked. "She… she… she…"

Mum had started laughing now. Em was already halfway off her chair laughing, because Dad's giggles are the most infectious thing in the world. Our dog Rascal crept out of his basket and sat nervously by the back door as my whole family totally lost it.

"It's not funny," I said, my lips twitching. "It's…"

And then I joined in.

When we'd all got our breath back, me and Em cleared and washed the plates as Mum and Dad went next door to recover.

"What do you think we should do, Em?" I said,

drying the plates and stacking them in the cupboard. I was that desperate, I was turning to a seven-year-old footie freak for help.

"Write a letter," Em said, lining up the cutlery in the cutlery drawer. "No – write *two* letters. One from Ben to Jasmine, and one from Jasmine to Ben. You can be all sorry-sorry, lovey-lovey, I promise never to mention it again and all that. They'll never know the other person didn't write it, see?" She plonked the last fork in the drawer and flipped the tea towel over her shoulder. "It works in movies," she concluded.

I stared at her. Was this maybe the best idea I'd heard all day? "You're a genius, Emma!" I said, fighting the urge to sweep my little sister off the ground and kiss her.

"I know," Em said. Then she did one of her big show-off burps, which kind of spoiled the moment.

93

On Monday over dinner I pulled the letters I'd done on my computer that weekend out of my bag and spread them across the table so Lucy and Mel could see them. Mel made out she was still angry with me, but she started thawing when she realised that I had a plan to save our band from extinction.

"See?" I explained. "This one's from Ben, saying how sorry he is for laughing at Jasmine, and how pretty she is even with yoghurt on her nose. And this one's from Jasmine, saying sorry for running off."

Mel and Lucy studied the letters, giggling as they read the soppy stuff I'd added in.

"You can forge Ben's signature, can't you?" I said to Lucy hopefully. "And I'll just do a squiggle for Jasmine and hope Ben doesn't know what her handwriting looks like."

94

"They'll kill us if they find out…" said Lucy tentatively. "But I guess things can't get much worse…" She pulled out her pen and signed Ben's letter with a flourish, while I did the same with Jasmine's. Then we put them both in envelopes.

"We can put them in the Year Ten pigeonholes," Mel said, completely into my plan now. "And then I guess we just hope for the best."

"We've been doing a lot of that lately," Lucy sighed.

It's amazing how slowly time goes when you're desperate for it to speed by. Every time we moved between classrooms, I was on alert for Ben and Jasmine. Had they got the letters yet? Had they read them? And most importantly – did they believe them? A small part of my brain did the usual stuff: writing down homework, shooting evils at Summer

(who seemed to be smirking a whole lot more than normal), planning the band's outfits for the Battle and practising our song. But the rest of my head was completely caught up in the Ben and Jasmine drama. The big question was: did we still have a band?

"You wanna practise at mine now?" Mel asked as we headed out of school at the end of the day.

"What's the point without Ben and Jasmine?" Lucy said with a shrug.

"We've got to believe it'll work out," Mel said. "There's less than two weeks left until the gig, guys."

"How's your mum, Mel?" I asked, suddenly remembering.

Mel shook her head. "Not great," she said. "She was applying for a bunch of other jobs over the weekend."

"*Jasmine*," Lucy suddenly hissed in my ear.

I whirled around. Jasmine Harris was walking down the corridor, flanked by a couple of her mates.

"And Ben!" Mel squeaked, lurching to a halt as we saw Lucy's brother walking towards us from the opposite direction.

We slammed ourselves back against the lockers that lined the corridor.

"I want a word with you, Ben Hanratty," Jasmine said.

"Is that good?" Lucy whispered nervously as we watched Ben and Jasmine walking towards each other like cowboys in some kind of high-noon shoot-out. "It doesn't sound good."

Jasmine's two mates slid away from her side like well-oiled spacepods leaving the mother ship. Was it my imagination, or had the whole corridor gone quiet?

"Ew," said Mel, as Ben and Jasmine suddenly ran into each other's arms. "What is it with these two doing stuff so *publicly*?"

The corridor started cheering and whooping. Totally oblivious, Ben and Jasmine kissed. I tried not

97

to stare. Seeing them like that was doing something very weird to my stomach. I'd never kissed anyone. I wondered what it would feel like – and if I'd ever do it and *not even notice the whole school was watching?*

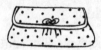

"OK," said Lucy as we got off the bus the next day. "I'm officially grossed out."

"It's all for the good of the band," Mel pointed out.

I was wishing I had little earflaps I could lower over my ears to cut out the smoochy noises going on behind us. Ben and Jasmine weren't going to let a little thing like arriving at school stop them now.

"I've rebooked practice room three for dinnertime today," Mel said. "Now we just have to tell the lovebirds to meet us there so we can do some serious work on our song. We've got *so* much to do."

"You'll tell Ben, won't you, Lu?" I said.

Lucy glanced back at her brother and Jasmine and shuddered. "No way am I interrupting *that*," she said. "I'll text him."

"By the way, how are you getting on with our outfits, Col?" asked Mel.

I'd been working out a scheme for our outfits since the weekend, and it was looking great. "Trust me," I said, tapping my nose. "I'm working on it."

And with that sorted, we made our way to our classroom. Summer pushed past us as we got to the door, making Mel lose her footing and bang into the wall.

"What *is* your problem, Summer?" I demanded. Summer Collins was really winding me up now.

Summer smirked at me. "*I'm* not the one with the problem," she said.

"I don't like the way Hannah and Shona laughed just then," I said to Mel in a low voice as we took our

seats. Something was going on with Summer, and it was making me nervous.

"Forget them," Mel said. "They're just jealous of our five-piece band." She said *five-piece band* extra loudly, just to make sure Summer could hear her. "With that and our brilliant song, Summer's little Fashionistas haven't got a hope in the Battle."

"Summer might have written a good song," I pointed out. Summer and her mates were certainly looking confident about *something*.

"Yeah," Lucy agreed.

"They haven't got an original idea in their heads," Mel scoffed. "You've only got to look at them to know that."

We gazed at the way Summer, Hannah and Shona had all done their hair in side ponytails today. I don't mean to be unkind, but Mel had a point.

So what exactly was Summer looking so pleased about?

100

We soon found out.

Most dinnertimes, if the weather's OK, the hall isn't too busy. But because of the rain today, it was heaving. Practically all the tables were full and we had to queue for ages to get our food.

"That's ten minutes gone from our rehearsal time," Mel said fretfully, banging her tray down on the last table we could find – the one right by the kitchens, which no one ever wants to sit at because of the smell. "Everyone eat fast, yeah?"

We all turned to gaze at where Jasmine was sitting on Ben's lap two tables down, feeding him bits of pasta and roaring with laughter. Eating like that was going to take *ages*. I was wondering how we could get their attention when Summer, Hannah and Shona stopped at the table in between us and Ben.

"I see you got your letters then," Summer said conversationally to Ben and Jasmine.

The food in my mouth turned to dust as Ben and Jasmine looked round at Summer in surprise. A bit of pasta was still hanging off Ben's lip.

"Only," Summer continued, "I guess no one told you that you didn't write them. They were from your tragic little band mates."

How—?

Summer shot me a look of blazing triumph. "You really shouldn't blab your plans all over the dinner hall, Coleen," she said. "I mean – anyone could be listening."

We just gawped at her in horror.

"Sorry about your *five-piece band*, Mel," Summer added silkily as Ben and Jasmine suddenly pushed away from each other. "Looks like you might just be down to three."

Eight

"OK," I began helplessly, holding up my hands towards Ben and Jasmine as Summer and her mates howled with laughter and wiggled off down the dinner hall. Lucy and Mel just sank their heads down on to the table as I spluttered: "We can explain, honest—"

"This had better be good," Jasmine said.

"We're listening," Ben said.

I couldn't read their faces at all.

"Right," I said, wetting my lips and darting a

frantic glance at my mates. But Lucy and Mel's heads were firmly in their hands. It looked like I was going to get the full blame here – smack between the eyes.

"Well," I began, "since it's totally clear to everyone in the school that you guys are nuts about each other, we just maybe gave you a *teensy* little nudge back together. You'd have got there in the end," I added hastily. "We just – didn't have time to wait, with the Battle of the Bands in just a couple of weeks, and... I mean," I continued, feeling a little bolder as they didn't howl me down, "you should be thanking us, right?"

"Thanking you," Ben repeated.

"Next you'll be telling us that you somehow set us up when we joined the band too?" Jasmine said.

Mel cleared her throat. "Funny you should say that," she mumbled.

"Are you really, *really* mad?" Lucy asked, peeping

timidly at her brother from between her fingers.

"It was my little sister's idea," I burst out, seeing all my plans for winning the Battle of the Bands going up in smoke, "and I know you're thinking: *what kind of idiot listens to a seven-year-old?* and you're probably right – but we were that desperate! And you're just dead good, both of you, and it was a real shame you didn't make it past the qualifiers, Ben…"

I tailed off. Ben and Jasmine both had these looks on their faces that reminded me of Dad when I was telling him about the pink yoghurt.

"Are you – laughing at me?" I asked doubtfully.

"Yup," said Mel, as Ben and Jasmine both fell about, holding their sides and totally wetting themselves. "I think they are, Col."

So much for Summer Collins' plan. Ben and Jasmine

thought it was the funniest thing ever. I guess that's love for you. We cracked on with our rehearsals, with Ben and Jasmine never wasting an opportunity to take the mick out of us for setting them up. I didn't care. The song was going well at last, and having my crush and his girlfriend laughing at me was a small price to pay.

"Summer's as sour as a lemon with toothache," Mel said gleefully as we finished rehearsals for the week on Friday dinnertime.

"Good," Lucy said. "First she nicked our song for the qualifiers, and then she tried to ruin our band for the final. I mean, how would she like it if we did that to *her*?"

That set me thinking. Summer had got away with too much since this whole Battle thing began – not to mention the way she'd set me up at the fashion show that time. Payback was way overdue.

"Have either of you heard Summer's band practising this week?" I asked thoughtfully.

Mel pulled a face. "Yes, worse luck," she said. "I'm telling you, they were like three cats in a bag. *You push my buttons, baby,*" she started singing in a squeaky Summer voice, "*I love you true, you push my buttons baby, I love youuu...* Lame or what?"

"Makes her sound like a pedestrian crossing," Lucy giggled.

I almost fell over as a brilliant idea whooshed through me, tingling through to my fingertips. It was a blinder.

"I know how we can get Summer back!" I squealed. "She's always stealing our ideas, right?" Mel and Lucy nodded.

"So," I grinned, "let's give her something to steal."

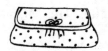

The last lesson of the week was IT with Mr Rat. Mr Rat's full name is Mr Ratnasinghe, but no one ever calls him that. He's a really laid-back teacher, and he doesn't mind much what we get up to during his lessons, so long as we got our work done.

Just like we'd hoped, Summer and her mates had already bagged terminals F, G and H, which stand by the window. The worst ones – the ones with dodgy mouses and scratched keyboards – stand in the next row, just in front of Summer. No one ever wants to sit there, which was part of the plan.

"Mr Rat?" I said in a low voice as we all shuffled into the classroom. "Can we sit at terminals N, O and P?"

Mr Rat looked surprised. Well, as surprised as Mr Rat ever gets, which involves him raising his eyebrows two millimetres. "You want to sit there?" he said. "Go ahead."

This was Mel's cue. "Oh, Mr *Raat*!" she wailed at the top of her voice.

Summer and her mates looked up.

"I can't *believe* you're making us sit there!" I added in my loudest, grumpiest voice.

Mr Rat looked confused. "But you—" he began.

"OK, whatever," I snapped, cutting Mr Rat off and making a big deal out of flouncing towards the terminals with Mel and Lucy following me. Poor Mr Rat looked totally flummoxed.

Phase one of our plan had worked like a dream. Now it was time for phase two.

"But I want to wear the yellow one," Mel said loudly to me as we worked through the spreadsheet on our screens. "It'll look better for the gig than the red."

"Ssshh," Lucy hissed, pointing really obviously over her shoulder at Summer.

You could hear Summer's ears flapping like mad behind us. Biting my lip so I didn't laugh and give the game away, I whispered loudly: "No – we'll do it

like we said. Green for Lu, Red for you, Mel, and I'll take the yellow. Got it?"

Then we bent our heads over our work and concentrated on not giggling for the rest of the lesson. There was no way Summer hadn't heard us. But would she take the bait?

We'd arranged for a long rehearsal at Jasmine's place on Saturday morning. I'm always interested in other people's houses (nosey, Em would say), so it was brilliant seeing where Jasmine lived. It's this old house right on the edge of Hartley, with a rambling garden full of apple trees and clutter and an old garage at the bottom where Jasmine plays guitar and hangs out with her mates.

"Help yourselves," Jasmine said, switching on the garage light and pointing to a tray of biscuits and fruit beside a kettle.

"Cool," Mel gasped.

It *was* pretty cool. Jasmine had these two old couches in one corner of the garage arranged around a packing crate covered with a bright cloth that acted as a table. She'd decorated the couches with cushions, and paintings and drawings were stuck all over the bare concrete walls. A collection of random stuff lay scattered over the table: a couple of pens, a big black watch, several CDs out of their boxes and sheaves of guitar music all heavily scribbled over with a pencil. At the far end of the garage was a knackered old drum kit – "My mum's," Jasmine explained – and more packing crates, this time with cushions on top for sitting on.

"Sorry about the mess." Jasmine looked quite embarrassed as she cleared the top of the packing-crate table.

"This is wicked," I said, gazing around. Em would be *dead* jealous if I had a place like this.

Ben was already at the drum kit, testing the cymbals. "Ready when you are," he said, and launched into the intro of our song as we all scrambled into position.

We had the first verse down just right. But the second one started giving us problems.

"One more time," Mel said, after we'd messed it up twice.

"*The sea, the sea,*" we sang obediently, "*the sea and you, the sea can see that you're untrue...*"

"Sorry," Jasmine said, looking angry with herself as she mucked up in the same place again. "It's just that funny rhythm there..."

"Keep going," Ben called over the pounding drums.

"*You left the sand just like you planned,*" we went on, "*your life got messed, outta hand – you didn't, didn't stay in reach of paths that take you to the beach, ooh... Who's sorry now? Who's sorry now?*"

Ben was having a bit of difficulty with the last two lines, which were supposed to build up and repeat after a skipped beat. I stood by the drums and went over it with him, thinking dreamily how nice he smelled, while Jasmine hunched, frowning over her guitar, and Mel and Lucy went to sit down on the packing-crate stools.

"Whoa!" Mel shouted, sliding off the packing crate she'd been sitting on as the wood broke and splintered underneath her.

We all rushed over to help Mel up.

"Jasmine, I'm really sorry..." Mel turned bright red with embarrassment as we stared at the mess of wood and sawdust on the floor.

"Don't worry about it," Jasmine said, hunkering down to check out the contents of the packing crate. "It's just this dumb elephant of Mum's inside. She hates it but can't be bothered to get rid of it, so it just

113

lives in here. Too bad you didn't break it and all, Mel."

More sawdust slid out of the broken packing crate. Suddenly, we could all see a red, blue and white ceramic elephant's trunk. It looked familiar.

"I don't believe it," Mel said. "It looks just like—"

"—your mum's fireplace elephant," me and Lucy finished Mel's sentence at the same time.

Ben and Jasmine watched us with puzzled expressions as we all fell to the ground and started pulling away the rest of the sawdust and packing materials, revealing the elephant in its full trumpeting glory. It was a perfect match for Mrs Palmer's favourite ornament in the whole world.

"Did you say your mum hated this?" Mel said, scrambling to her feet and swinging round to Jasmine.

"Loathes it," Jasmine said.

"Do you think maybe – I could have it?" Mel asked breathlessly.

Jasmine started to laugh. "Mum'll think it's Christmas if you take it," she grinned. "Saves her a trip to the dump!"

Nine

I don't know how we managed it, but an hour later, me, Mel and Lucy were heaving Jasmine's elephant – we'd decided to call her Nelly – off the bus and staggering towards Mel's block of flats.

"Don't anyone dare drop Nelly now," Mel begged, sweat breaking out on her forehead as she struggled backwards down the pavement. "We didn't go through an hour of sore arms for her to end up in pieces on the road, right?"

We sidled carefully into the stairwell.

116

"Nice elephant," said a bloke we met on the stairs. "Where d'you get it? A jumbo sale?"

"Ha ha," Mel said in a sour voice as he headed on past us, laughing his head off.

"And thanks for offering to help us carry it!" I added sarcastically.

"Plonker," muttered Lucy – which is about as rude as Lucy ever gets.

When we reached Mel's front door on the third floor, we put Nelly down with a massive sigh of relief. My arms felt really weird, like my hands were going to float up to the sky all by themselves.

"I hope your mum likes Nelly after all that," said Lucy, collapsing against the wall as Mel fiddled with her keys.

"She'll love her," Mel said, managing to look both dead pleased and totally knackered at the same time. "She's been looking for a matching one for the

117

fireplace for *ever*! I still can't believe we found Nelly. I honestly—"

The door opened and Mel's mum reached out to sweep Mel into a hug. Me and Lucy glanced at each other in surprise. She hadn't even *looked* at Nelly yet!

"I got a new job!" Mrs Palmer said in excitement, kissing Mel all over the top of her head. "It's an extra three pounds an hour, and it's right on the bus route! They just rang to tell me!"

"Wow, that's brilliant, Mum!" Mel gasped. "Looks like your cheering-up present just turned into a celebration present!" She stepped aside and revealed Nelly with a flourish and a grin that went from ear to ear. "Ta-da!"

And I think the whole block heard Mrs Palmer's scream of delight.

Every time we saw Summer and her mates in the last week leading up to the Battle of the Bands final, we made this big thing of saying "Shh!" to each other, like we'd been discussing something really secret – even if we'd just been talking about homework or last night's TV or whatever. We also used the words "red", "yellow" and "green" as often as we could, knowing that Summer was desperate for more details about our "secret" look for Saturday's show.

"Enough about Summer Collins," Jasmine snapped at our last school dinnertime rehearsal the day before the gig. "What about *our* look? Or have you been too busy doing one of your special *set-ups* to remember you've got a real band to style?"

"Give over, Jas," Ben said as me and the others stopped giggling about Summer and turned to look guiltily at Jasmine.

Jasmine had been in a funny mood most of the week.

119

I hoped she wasn't building up to one of her mega flounce-offs. We were so close now, I could almost feel the cool metal of the trophy between my fingers.

"I've got the *best* look for us," I said, keen to head Jasmine off at the mardy crossroads. "Don't worry about Summer. We're going – *pink*!"

"Oh no, we're not," Ben said at once.

"Hear me out," I begged. "We're talking *hot* pink, almost red, right? I'm doing a T-shirt for Ben. Me, Lucy and Mel can all wear pink tops with black footless tights – and Jasmine? Is there any way you can get some hot-pink skinny jeans? The rest is up to you – but the pink touches pull us together as a band."

"I'm *not* wearing pink," Ben repeated stubbornly.

"Don't be so boring, Ben," said Jasmine, fiddling with her guitar. "It'll look great. Topshop have pink skinny jeans in at the minute. I've been after a pair

120

for ages. Mum'll give me some money if I tell her they're for the Battle."

Ben went into a sulk and didn't say anything else for the rest of the rehearsal. He just hit the drums so hard that the walls shook around us.

"Is it just me," said Mel as we wound up and agreed to meet at Lucy's place tomorrow afternoon for the dress rehearsal, "or are those two going off the boil?"

We watched Ben stalking off down the corridor. Jasmine was making no attempt to catch him up.

"Don't say that," I said anxiously. "We can't have them splitting up and leaving the band, not now we're so close to the gig."

And not now I've borrowed one of Dad's white T-shirts, tied it up in a bunch of rubber bands and stuck it in a bucket of pink dye either, I thought privately to myself.

121

"Coleen," Dad said, standing in his PJs on Saturday morning and frowning at the dye-bucket that was sat by the back door. "Please tell me that's not blood in there."

"Gross," Em mumbled through a mouthful of chewed-up Weetabix.

"Course not, Dad," I said, steering him back towards the breakfast table. "Here you go. Look, a lovely cup of tea for you. And I've done Marmite on toast, just how you like it."

"It *is* blood, isn't it?" Dad asked suspiciously. "That's why you're being nice."

"Come on," I protested. "Where am I going to get a whole bucket of blood from?"

"Your vampire victims," said Dad in a ghoulish voice. "You must've bitten half the street to get that

122

much in there. Come to think of it, I haven't seen Mum this morning."

"Mum's at the supermarket, as you well know," I said, rolling my eyes.

"Stop talking about blood or I'm gonna BE SICK," Em announced.

When Dad and Em had gone for their usual Saturday-morning footie training, I covered the floor with newspaper, put on Mum's rubber gloves and carefully pulled Dad's T-shirt out of the dye. Then I pulled off the rubber bands that had been holding the tee in place.

"Yes!" I said in triumph as I stared at the coolest hot-pink tie-dye pattern you ever saw. I bundled it into the washing machine along with a ton of salt like the instructions said, and set the machine to its hottest temperature. Ben was going to *love* it!

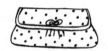

Mel and Lucy whooped as I held up the finished T-shirt for Ben to admire over at Lucy's that afternoon.

"What do you think?" I asked Ben.

Ben looked like he had a right cob on today. "It's OK," he said in a grumpy voice, and took it off me.

"Ignore Ben," Jasmine said. She was already wearing her outfit: new pink skinnies with a bright red T-shirt and these brilliant stacked-heel shoes on the bottom. "It's cool. How did you do the pattern?"

"Secret," I grinned. "So, d'you like it, Ben?"

OK, so maybe I shouldn't have asked his opinion twice.

"I *said* it was OK, didn't I?" Ben snapped.

"Let's all get changed and meet back down here in ten minutes," said Mel, trying to jolly things along.

"What's eating Ben this week?" I asked Lucy as we all went into her room to get changed.

"The usual," said Lucy.

124

"Not Dave again?" Mel gasped.

Lucy nodded. "Ben's heard more rumours. He doesn't want to kick off about it because Jasmine got so mad at him last time, but it's doing his head in."

"Just so long as he can keep it together till the end of tonight's gig," I said, pulling on my footless tights beneath a long pink blouse of Mum's that I had snipped here and there and pulled in at the waist with a belt. "Come on, is everyone ready? We look wicked!"

Me and my mates stood arm in arm and admired ourselves in Lucy's wardrobe mirror. We looked brilliant. And just as I thought, our footless tights pulled everything together like a dream.

"Bounce Back rocks!" I shouted and punched the air.

"Yay!" Mel and Lucy squealed.

Bounce Back rocked all right. But if we'd known what was coming, we maybe wouldn't have yelled quite so loudly.

There were now only a couple of hours left till the warm-up and the Battle, and my nerves were seriously starting to kick in. There was just one thing for it. Chocolate.

"Anyone fancy going into town?" I asked the others as we finished carefully packing away our costumes at the end of the dress rehearsal. Jasmine had wriggled off early with promises of seeing us at the Town Hall at a quarter to six, and Ben had stomped off to his bedroom where he was now playing heavy metal really loudly.

"You're on," said Mel.

"I'm getting dead nervous," Lucy mumbled.

I knew what she meant. But as predicted, a chunky chocolate bar on a Hartley town bench cheered us all up no end, and we started to get seriously excited.

126

"Fame," I said dreamily as we planned a gorgeous future for Bounce Back once we'd got our hands on the trophy. I closed my eyes between bites of chocolate, picturing it all. "Magazine front covers…"

"A massive recording contract and a sponsorship deal with Cadbury's…" Mel added, and we squealed with delight at the thought of all the free chocs a deal like that would mean.

"Summer and her mates…" said Lucy.

I opened my eyes in confusion. What did Summer and her mates have to do with the future of our band?

Summer Collins, Hannah Davies and Shona Mackinnon had just appeared around the corner. They were carrying shopping bags and arguing about something – which meant they hadn't seen us yet.

"Behind the bench!" I ordered the others, thinking fast.

A few passers-by looked weirdly at us as we slid off

the bench and crept round behind it. Summer and her mates were getting closer now, and we could hear them talking.

"...*much* better on me," Summer was saying. "Besides, Coleen's wearing it, and as she's the leader of *that* sad little crew, it's only right that I get it."

Behind our bench we gazed at each other in delight. Proof at last that Summer had fallen into our trap, hook, line and mascara!

"Are you calling us sad?" Hannah said in confusion.

Summer tutted in annoyance. "You can be dead thick sometimes, Hannah. I'm saying that *I'm* wearing the yellow, right? That'll really show Coleen who's queen of the scene! You can take the green and Shona can do red."

"Are we definitely on before them?" Shona asked, trailing behind the other two as they walked right past our bench, their shoes millimetres from our noses.

"Only, this is gonna look dead stupid if they go first."

"I *told* you, dimwit," Summer hissed, her voice fading away now. "I've got the running order. We're sixth and they're eighth…"

We all peered over the top of the bench, happily watching as the Fashionistas trotted on and out of sight.

"You know what?" Mel said. "I was looking forward to tonight before. But now – I can't wait."

And I knew exactly what she meant.

Ten

"**S**orry I'm late," I gasped, rushing into the Town Hall at ten past six with my gear bouncing on my back in a plastic bag.

There was loads of activity everywhere, with guys in black T-shirts and headsets lifting massive amps around the stage and setting up light rigs that flashed through all the wicked colours I remembered from the Bubbly gig. The atmosphere was nervy and exciting with all the qualified bands pacing around and looking scared, waiting to be called for their sound-check.

There were twelve bands in total from all over town, including Summer and her Fashionistas and the other band from our qualifier, Thrash Bunnies. And it looked like we weren't the only band to have changed our lineup. Standing with the Thrash Bunnies was none other than Dave Sheekey, tuning his guitar and adjusting his new dark-blue band T-shirt.

"Where have you been, Col?" Mel demanded. "I said to meet here at quarter to!"

"Three lots have already done their sound-checks," Jasmine said angrily. She was as jumpy as a frog on springs. "We're dead lucky we haven't been called yet."

"Long story," I panted, hugely relieved that I hadn't missed our sound-check. I wanted everything to be perfect tonight, and everyone knows how important sound-checks are for adjusting the volume on microphones and all that.

131

"So what's your excuse?" Lucy said.

I'd got home after seeing Summer in town to find Mum standing in the hall with her hands on her hips, wanting to know why her whole white wash had gone pink: knickers, socks, all mine and Em's school shirts, Dad's work overalls and Em's football shorts included. After my stuttered explanation I got the Questions: how could I have forgotten to leave Mum a note telling her I'd used her machine for dyeing? How could I have dyed Dad's best white T-shirt without asking him first? Then Mum got me at the sink with bleach, stain removers and instructions to come nowhere near the table for tea until everything was white again.

"And *then* she said I had to buy Dad a new T-shirt and walk Rascal for the next fortnight, starting with right after tea, and she didn't care if I was late for the sound-check; I was lucky to be allowed anywhere

132

near the Town Hall tonight, blah, blah," I finished.

"You idiot," Mel said, and started to grin.

"Bounce Back to the stage please," came a voice over the microphone, making us jump out of our skins.

With chattering teeth, we all walked up the hall.

"Good luck, mate," Dave said hopefully as Ben brushed past him.

Ben grunted something in reply which was either "Good luck yourself" or something a whole lot ruder. It was difficult to tell.

"It's good that Dave and Ben are talking again," Lucy said to me as we took our positions and tried not to feel too freaked out by the huge space of the Town Hall laying out in front of us.

"That depends what they're saying to each other," I said, glancing back at Dave.

The sound-check went fine. It was the craziest feeling in the world, hearing your own voice

133

booming back to you through a massive sound system. It made me realise, maybe for the first time, just what we'd got ourselves into here. There wasn't time to do the whole song – just the start and the finish. But it left my head ringing all the same.

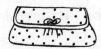

Hartley's Battle of the Bands was due to start at seven o'clock. People came flooding in as soon as the stage technicians said they were done with the sound-checks, and the Town Hall was filling up as fast as a welly in deep water. I gasped as I saw Deena from Bubbly take her seat with the rest of the judging panel at the front of the hall – and then I spotted my folks.

"You made it!" I said in relief, hurrying over to them as they came in the door. My eyes slid guiltily over Em's still faintly pink England footie shirt.

134

"Don't say a word," Em growled.

"We wouldn't have missed it," said Mum, "however daft you've been."

"I *will* get you a new T-shirt, Dad," I promised, giving everyone quick hugs.

"'Course you will," said Dad comfortably. "Just like you'll get me a cup of tea in bed every day for the next week."

"Good luck, Coleen love," Nan said, patting me on the cheek with one warm little hand as the voice on the microphone summoned everyone to their seats.

The lights dimmed as I plonked into my reserved place beside Mel and Lucy. My heart was really going now. That special hush fell, the one you always get before a show, and Thrash Bunnies took to the stage.

"They were much better than I remembered at the qualifiers," Mel whispered across at me as everyone cheered at the end of their set.

"Looks like Dave was a good extra," I whispered back.

Jasmine looked like she was about to agree with me, but something stopped her – probably the thought of Ben hearing her saying nice stuff about his supposed love rival. I noticed she and Ben weren't holding hands like normal and hoped it was just nerves.

We all listened as the panel – including Deena – said a few words on what they thought of Thrash Bunnies' performance. They were pretty complementary. I closed my eyes and really, really hoped Deena would say some nice things about us.

The next four bands were scarily good. From where we were sitting, we could see Deena's multicoloured hair as she bent towards another judge for a chat, then congratulated the band members on their excellent performances. Were we anywhere near good enough for this competition?

 136

"Look out, world," Mel said happily. "It's the Fashionistas."

We watched as Summer, Hannah and Shona lined up on the stage. Their make-up was even worse than it had been at the qualifiers. This was better than good. This was totally *perfect.*

Ben bent towards us. "Is it just me," he said in a low voice, "or do they look like a row of traffic lights?"

I nodded, frantically biting back a mad desire to giggle as Shona, Summer and Hannah lined up, holding out their hands in front of them. Their backing track started up.

"*Walk to me,*" Summer began, beckoning with one finger, "*come this way, cross the line, hear me say...*"

"Wait for the green man first," Mel sang out cheerfully.

A couple of people near us started chuckling as they saw the traffic-light resemblance in their

costumes. Once you'd seen it, it was impossible to take the song seriously.

"*You push my buttons, baby,*" Hannah and Shona started grinding away in their red and green dresses. "*I love you true, you push my buttons, baby...*"

"Bus coming through!" roared a joker somewhere further down the hall.

"*I love youuu...*"

The Fashionistas pressed on valiantly, although it was beginning to dawn on them that something was going deeply wrong. The laughter began to spread as Summer's lyrics pushed the joke to heights I had only dreamed of. By the time they reached: "*Gimme the green light, green light for your love,*" they couldn't make themselves heard over the riotous laughter flooding the hall.

"Walk, don't walk!" chanted the crowd in delight. "Walk, don't walk!"

Summer stopped singing, completely purple with rage. "I hate you all!" she screeched, and ran off the stage with Hannah and Shona running after her. The hall erupted in tumultuous applause.

"That was the funniest thing I've ever seen," said Dave Sheekey, wiping his eyes and leaning his arm over the back of his seat as he turned to us.

"Right on," Mel sighed in complete satisfaction, high-fiving Lucy.

I couldn't speak. "Hoohoo," I gasped weakly as Deena and the other judges struggled to find something nice to say about the Fashionistas. I thought I was about to die with the joyful pain of it all. "Hoohoohoohahahoo…"

"Where's your watch, Dave?" said Ben.

Dave looked surprised. He glanced at his bare wrist. "Dunno," he said. "Must've left it somewhere."

For some reason, my giggles dried up. This wave of

tension ripped through me as I looked at Dave, and then at Ben, and then at Jasmine, who was sitting totally still.

"Bounce Back?" A stage technician was hunkering down beside our row. "Backstage, please."

Ben leaped up and barged past us all.

"Wait," said Jasmine, struggling out of her seat.

"Where's the fire, Ben?" Lucy complained as we followed Ben, Jasmine and the techie down a little corridor that took us backstage. Jasmine kept trying to grab Ben's arm, but he shook her off each time. I watched them with this growing feeling of doom.

"I don't think it's a fire we should be worrying about," Mel said, echoing my thoughts. "What was that about Dave's watch?"

"Ten minutes to change, and then you're on," said the techie, leaving us in this little dressing room.

I felt sick as the image of Dave Sheekey's big black watch swam into my head. I knew exactly where I

140

had seen it. It had been lying on the messy packing-crate table at Jasmine's place. *Which meant Dave had been there.* Like me, Ben must've spotted it – and then forgotten all about it till he saw Dave's bare wrist. Suddenly, the so-called rumour was looking less like a rumour, and more like…

"Ben?" Jasmine was saying. "Listen, don't do anything crazy, OK?"

Ben was ignoring her, pulling on his tie-dye T-shirt and black jacket in silence. His face was like thunder.

"Er," said Lucy in confusion, "what's going on, guys?"

"Two minutes!" went the tannoy over our heads. "Bounce Back, this is your two-minute call."

"*We*'re going on," Mel declared, dragging on her footless tights. "Come on – my mum's out there waiting to see us, and so's everyone else's folks. Let's talk about whatever the problem is after, yeah? We've got a show to do."

141

Dumbly I fixed my hair and pulled my black trilby on over the top with shaky fingers. We were about to hit the stage with a time-bomb on drums. I was so spooked at the thought of what Ben might do in front of hundreds of people that I didn't even smile at the sight of a dumbstruck Summer, Shona and Hannah halfway down the corridor as they took in our totally un-traffic-light-like outfits.

"Bounce Baaack!" went the announcer. The audience cheered. We were on.

Ben marched over to the drums and started attacking them almost before we'd all got in position. Jasmine turned her back on him and started into her guitar line with a new and scary energy.

"*The sea, the sea, the sea and me,*" we began. Mel and me kept glancing back nervously at Ben, and then at Jasmine, and then back again like we were at some nightmare tennis match. If it hadn't been for Lucy,

we'd have lost our way before the end of the first verse. Ben was belting his drums like a maniac. It was like the qualifiers all over again, but on a much bigger scale. And we were right in the middle of it!

"*The sea, the sea, the sea and you,*" we sang on into the second verse, praying that we could make it to the end before meltdown.

Ben started joining in. "*The sea can see that you're untrue,*" he belted out, pointing one drumstick at Jasmine's back.

Mel, Lucy and me ploughed on helplessly. "*You left the sand just like you planned...*"

"*Who's sorry now?*" Ben roared at Jasmine. "*WHO'S SORRY NOW, YOU SILLY—*"

We tried to drown Ben out with even louder words. But as loud as we went, he sang even louder. Jasmine was hunched over her guitar with tears pouring down her face, but was still just about

holding on to the tune. I realised we were seriously overdoing it and sounding like a whole lot of wailing cats, but there was nothing else we could do.

"Dance... dance routine," I nudged at Mel and Lucy, hoping that the dance steps we'd put together for the qualifier would distract everyone from Ben. We hadn't planned to use the routine now that we were more of a rock band, so none of us had practised. We ended up banging and bumping into each other like nobody's business. The whole thing was a *total* mess.

We didn't win. But you know what? I was just so relieved to get off that stage in one piece that I didn't care. Being twelve sucks a lot of the time, but if being fourteen means dealing with the kind of mega love disasters we'd seen with Ben and Jasmine since starting our band, I'll take twelve any day. And at least

Ben Hanratty was single again and available for his old starring role in my daydreams...

Besides, I told myself as I got ready for bed that night. *Look on the bright side.* OK, so I still had to walk Rascal for weeks, spend all my future pocket money on a T-shirt for Dad, and generally keep my head down round ours for a bit. But we'd had some amazing feedback from Deena after our performance. She loved the song – both the music and my lyrics! Mind you, she also said the guitarist could do with cheering up and that we should get rid of the angry drummer. But the big thing was: my total heroine Deena had told us we were cool. And what could be better than that?

Em's wrong about winning being everything.

Rockin Pocket Purse

Don't throw away old denim jeans or shorts. Recycle them instead to make a super-cute bag!

ASK AN ADULT BEFORE YOU GET SEWING!

HAVE FUN!

You will need:

★ An old pair of jeans/shorts

★ Sharp scissors

★ A needle and thread

★ Press stud (popper)

★ Badges/brooches/buttons/

sequins/beads (optional)

PLEASE TAKE CARE WITH BOTH THE NEEDLE AND THE SCISSORS!

Step 1

Cut off the back pockets from an old pair of jeans.

Step 2

Hold the pockets together right side out and carefully sew around the edge, leaving the top section open. You could use a brightly coloured thread so the stitching stands out.

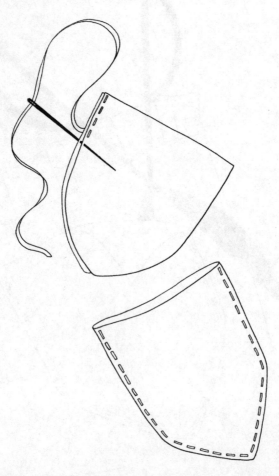

Step 3

Sew the popper sections to either side of the inside opening.

Step 4

Sew the ends of a length of strong ribbon to the inside edges of the bag to make a strap.

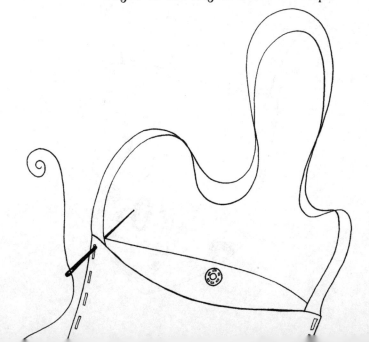

Step 5

Attach badges, brooches, buttons - any decorations you like.

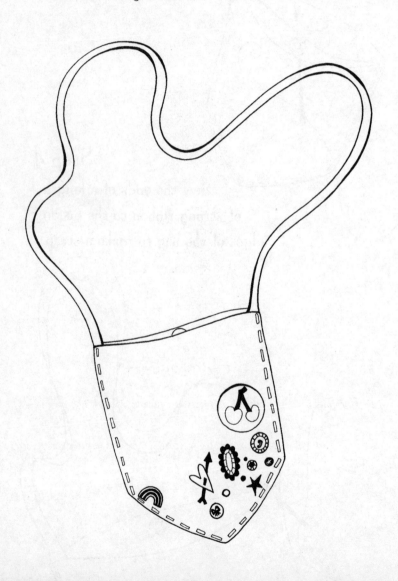

VOILÀ!

YOUR ROCKIN POCKET PURSE!

You could also try..

⭐ Cutting a long strip of denim to make a matching strap.

⭐ Plaiting coloured ribbons for a multicoloured effect.

⭐ Using a pretty scarf instead.

OUT NOW!

Book Four

Sun, Sand & Sequins

Going on a sizzling summer holiday? Need to
look beachtastic? Then maybe I can help. I'm
Coleen and I love fashion, friends and having fun.

The hotel owner's gorgeous son has asked me
out, but my suitcase is lost in transit! Help!
Nothing to wear on my first ever date....

Turn the page for a sneak preview...

HarperCollins *Children's Books*

OK, so holiday packing can be a struggle. Especially when you've got a mountain of clothes and shoes – not to mention an iPod, a camera and a hairdryer – to pack into a case roughly the size of a box of tissues. Oh, and did I mention that this particular suitcase is pink with gold sparkles?

"Mum!" I complained as Mum got my suitcase down from the loft and put it on my bed. "I can't take this on holiday. I'll get laughed off the beach!"

"You loved it when you were seven, and I'm sure you can love it again, Coleen," said Mum.

I sighed and flipped the case open. Then I packed my favourite summer shoes: a pair of sparkly sandals covered in silver sequins. They fitted – with about three millimetres left over. "But I'll never get everything in!" I wailed, looking at the other six pairs that I'd lined up on my bedroom floor.

"What do you need seven pairs of shoes for?" Dad

asked, stopping at my room and staring at my packing. There was something bright orange draped over his arm. "We're going for a *beach* holiday, Coleen – tomorrow, ideally, though at the rate you're going you won't be packed until Tuesday. Are you planning to paddle in a different pair of shoes every day?"

I rolled my eyes at him. Dads don't *get* shoes. "What's that?" I asked, eyeing the orange thing on Dad's arm.

"Ta-da!" Dad announced, unfurling the most disgusting pair of orange swimming trunks I'd ever seen and flapping them at me. "What do you think?"

"The fish in the sea'll think you're a giant Wotsit, Dad," I advised. "Think again."

"At least you lot won't lose me at the hotel pool," Dad joked, folding up his shorts again.

"Believe me, Dad, we will," I muttered as Dad went off to help Mum squeeze everything into their old black case on wheels. "As quickly as we can."

My little sister, Em, wandered into my room and flopped down on the bed. As usual, she looked a total mess. Football strip (badly in need of a wash), football socks and a pair of trackie bottoms with holes in the knees, not to mention a gap in her front teeth where a tooth had just dropped out.

"And there was me, thinking seven-year-old girls wore pink all day long," I sighed.

"Yuck," said Em, as I knew she would. Needless to say, her suitcase had the emblem of her favourite footie team, Marshalswick Park, on it.

"Get out of here, Em," I begged, trying to decide between three different T-shirts. "Haven't you got packing to do?"

"All done," Em smirked.

"What?" I shrieked, dropping my tees. "But you only started about five minutes ago!"

Em shrugged. "Cozzie, T-shirts, shorts, sandals, latest football mag, autograph book because footballers go to the Algarve and you never know, toothbrush," she recited. "Didn't take long."

"What about knickers?" I demanded.

Em wrinkled her forehead. "Oh yeah," she said, getting off my bed, "I'd better stick in a couple of pairs."

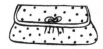

Holidays in my family usually go like this. Mum goes on at Dad for weeks to book something. The holidays get closer. Dad doesn't do anything until the last minute, and then he grabs the cheapest thing he sees, which nearly always has flights leaving at four o'clock in the morning. Mum's left running around like a mad thing, getting Nan to take Rascal our dog and vacuuming behind the couch. Well, this time, Dad has totally outdone himself. He booked us a week in the

Algarve this afternoon – and we are getting a taxi to the airport before sunrise tomorrow morning.

"Heaven knows what this place is going to be like," Mum grumbled as we all grabbed a bite to eat before what was going to be the shortest night's sleep in history.

"It's the Algarve, Trish," Dad said soothingly. "Sea, sand and plenty of sun. I tell you, I can spot the good ones a mile off. When have I ever been wrong?"

"Well," Mum started, "how about that time we went to Croatia and the hotel hadn't even been built? Or the trip to Brittany that turned out to be a trip to Britain, which I didn't want to visit because *I already lived there*? Or–"

"Well, this one's going to be different," Dad interrupted hastily. "Trust me."

Em and I shared a look. We'd believe *that* once we got there.

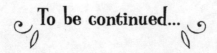

To be continued...